KILLING

YOU

AGAIN

LAURIANE
POVEY

First published in Great Britain 2017
ISBN: 978-0-9928951-0-5

Published by
The Wacky Wordshop.
40 Emmerson Way
Hadleigh,
Suffolk
IP7 6DJ

http://thewackywordshop.co.uk

Cover illustration Copyright:
Josh Povey

Printed and bound by:
Amazon CreateSpace

Acknowledgements.

The publication of Killing You Again is many years later than I initially anticipated. It feels such a long time ago that I was writing the first draft during maths lessons at school. The story has undergone major changes since, and I hope "Killing You Again" has been worth the wait. I know I'm excited to finally see it as a finished book.

My first thank you must go to my maths teacher, Mr Quinn, who helped me achieve an A* in Maths in Year 10 which meant I could spend much of my time in Year 11 maths classes writing this book.

As always, I send a massive thank you to Brice, my publisher, for continuing to have faith in my writing and for his endless patience despite the time it has taken to actually get this book into print.

To Pav, my boyfriend, thank you for the many hours spent editing and all the helpful suggestions you made despite being so busy with your own studies.

Mum, your proof reading skills are first class but most of all, I want to say thank you for your unwavering support and belief in me.

Most importantly, I thank you, the reader, for picking up my book.

I hope you enjoy,

Lauriane.

Chapter 1

I'd been watching them for some time, knowing I'd get the sack if my manager caught me. I took my phone from my back pocket regardless, concealing it behind the booking table I was standing at. I wanted a good shot. I needed evidence if any woman was to believe her husband was cheating on her, and wouldn't have a better opportunity. The restaurant was slowing down for the night and they'd finished eating. They could leave any minute and I wanted the slimy bastard caught. I turned off my phone flash and took a couple of shots. The photos weren't brilliant, only the back of her head but his face clearly visible, plus, it was clear they were holding hands across the table. Besides, Lynette would have no reason not to believe me.

Five minutes later my boss asked me to collect the bill for table nine … *their* table. Up until then I'd successfully avoided contact with Declan, and I knew he hadn't noticed me … his eyes were glued to the cleavage opposite him. I approached the table professionally, (I didn't want to kick up a fuss and lose my job) waiting to see if he recognised me. We made eye contact. He said nothing, his face impassive. After waiting on another table I headed for the cleaning cupboard next to the toilets. I was aware he'd been watching me sorting out the bill. I tried not to look at him but felt his felt his eyes tracking me. I was opening the cupboard door when I heard the door catch behind me. In a second a hand held my wrist tightly.

"Laura, is it?"

"Lorna." I corrected him and turned to face him, letting go of the cupboard handle. His face was centimetres from mine in the dark, small corridor. I felt very uncomfortable.

"Lynette won't be happy when she finds out," I said, shrugging free of his grip around my wrist.

"And how will she ever know?" He snarled. I took my phone out of my pocket and showed him the picture I'd taken.

"Delete it!" he demanded.

"No. Lynette is a good person. She deserves the truth. Deserves better than you." He made a grab for the phone. I stepped back and fled into the 'ladies', hoping he wouldn't follow me. I was wrong. He barged open the door behind me and grabbed my arm. I gripped onto my phone as tight as possible but he was stronger. He snatched it from me and hurled it against

1

he wall. Its case flew off and bits of phone fell onto the floor. He picked up the bits and dropped them into the toilet.

"What proof now?" He smiled. Rage boiled inside me. "And if I see you anywhere near my wife it won't only be the phone that gets it." He walked back out into the restaurant. My phone had sunk to the bottom of the toilet bowl. I grabbed some paper towels, grimaced and plucked my phone out of the toilet. I dried it as best I could knowing it would be ruined regardless. Picking up the back part of the phone from the floor my mouth curled into a smirk. Alongside it lay the memory card.

Chapter 2

I looked at the image, enlarged on my computer. They were holding hands, openly. Even I could tell it was Declan so Lynette definitely would be able to. I printed it and put it in an envelope. Even though Lynette and Declan lived at number 4 on this street, practically opposite, I still used a stamp; he was bound to be suspicious of anything hand-delivered.

Lynette had often 'babysat' me when I was younger, especially while Mum and Dad were going through their rough patches. Since their divorce three years ago (and Mum being with Gary) we hadn't seen much of her but I still regarded her as a family friend. She volunteered at the charity shop in town, where I did work experience before getting the restaurant job. I never saw much of Declan. From what I could remember he was always 'working' or in his study. I didn't think much of him then, and now Lynette definitely deserved someone better.

Over the next couple of days I waited for something to happen, wondering when my letter would be delivered. I felt constantly anxious he'd do something hateful when he found out. He'd know instantly who'd sent it. Walking home from college later that week I turned off onto a side road whilst saying goodbye to a friend, when a black Jaguar pulled up alongside me. The window slid silently down.
"Lorna. Get in the car."
"No." I began walking away but he drove his car across my path and opened his door. I paused. This gave him the time to hop out of the car. I knew then I should have run back to the main road with people around, but he strode towards me. I felt myself shrink under his glare.
"Get in the car." He grabbed my shoulder, his thumb digging under my collar bone. Stupidly, I got in the car. He drove out of the estate in silence. I played with the zip on my coat, the thin metal often slipping out of my sweaty hands. I was praying he wouldn't take me far. He entered a side road on the outskirts of town. My anxiety was heightened by the silence. I was hoping the trip was just to scare me and kept telling myself that just because someone's having an affair doesn't make them a murderer. A short while later he turned left into a woodland car park, squeezing into a spot between two parked cars, so I couldn't open the passenger door. He unclipped his seat belt.

"You didn't do as you were told, Laura."

"Lorna." I snapped.

"Okay, as stupid as the name is, Lorna, you need to learn to keep your nose out of other people's business."

"And how is a trip to a country park going to teach me that?"

"Flippancy won't do you any favours." I stayed silent. After a moment he began again.

"I obviously didn't make myself clear enough at the restaurant. Don't mess with me. I've been offered a managing director's job in Singapore which comes with a penthouse apartment and a six-figure salary. You don't get that far in life by being nice. So, let me tell you this, keep your mouth shut and your nose out of my business and I might just keep my hands to myself." His face drew closer to mine, his eyes greedy. His left hand slipped onto my knee and his fingers crawled, spider-like, up my legs. "Do I make myself clear?" I said nothing and tried to push his hand off my leg. He tightened his grip on my thigh. "All you have to do is pretend you know nothing about me until Saturday. After that you'll never have to see me again, okay?" "Get off me!" His hand thumb slid to the inside my leg. I grabbed his hand with both of mine to try and shift his but his grip remained firm. I squirmed away until my back bumped the car door. He lent further in, ran his right hand through my hair, brushing my fringe back. His breath reeked of his sickly cologne. Up close, his face was lined with wrinkles, made more prominent by the smirk around his mouth.

"Please, get off me," I whimpered, my voice shaky, my heart pounding. "This time I will. If I catch you anywhere near the house ... next time you may not be so lucky." He started the car and reversed out of the car park.

"If you're moving to Singapore how come your house isn't for sale?" I asked. We were safely on the way home and my heart was beating normally again.

"You don't seriously think I'm taking my wife do you?"

"How would I know?" He ignored me.

"She's a fat, lazy cow, milking me for my money. I'm not having her scrounging off my wealth anymore." I'd have opened my mouth with some nasty retort but he'd pulled up in the pub car park down the road from my house, and I made sure I was out of the car the moment it stopped.

"If you breathe one word to anyone, I'll have your life. A stupid teenage girl is not ruining my life." I looked into his cold, brown eyes once more before slamming the door shut. I was shocked, livid and more than a little scared. I didn't let on to anyone at home what had happened. I'd made up my mind ... he wasn't going to blackmail me into silence. I could have told my mum or stepdad, or even the police, but I had no proof and didn't want to cause a fuss. I'd get back at him in my own way.

After college the next day I caught a bus into town and went into the charity shop where Lynette (who was busy) worked, had a quick chat with Bernice, who I knew from the time I'd volunteered there, then went over to Lynette busy putting out some womens' coats, thankful she was working today as I daren't go near the house.
"Hey." I called out to get her attention.
"Hi Lorna." She smiled. Maybe she was a bit chubby and didn't wear make up, but she had a warm smile and a lovely personality.
"You've done me a favour coming in today. I was going to pop over to your's to see your mum tonight but you've saved me a job. Declan is taking me on holiday to Singapore on Saturday and I was going to ask your mum to watch over the house." I didn't know what to say.
"Singapore?"
"Yeah. He's shown me photos of this posh apartment we're staying in. I'm so excited!" Her face beamed. I didn't want to burst her bubble.
"Didn't you get the letter with the photo in it?" *It must have arrived, why else had her husband all but kidnapped me the day before.*
"What letter? He opens all the post." *Damn. So she really was clueless. It now made sense why he still wanted me to keep my mouth shut.*
"I'm so sorry Lynette." *How the hell was I to tell her in public?*
"What's happened?" She was searching my face for answers.
"Declan was with another woman. He took her out for a meal in the restaurant I'm working at."
"He said he was going out for a business meal. The client must have been female, you've got it wrong."
"They were holding hands, and definitely not discussing business. I took a photo of them. Your husband threatened me but I posted the photo to you."
"He threatened you?" Her cheeks had lost their natural rosy colour.
"Yesterday he picked me up from college in his car and told me to stay away. He said he was moving to Singapore on Saturday ... and you

weren't going with him." I spoke quietly, feeling nervous and guilty at breaking the news to her here. She didn't need to know all the gruesome details just yet.

"You've got it wrong. I've seen our plane tickets."

"I've got the photo on my computer."

"It was probably nothing."

"Lynette, please, believe me. He's got a new job in Singapore."

"Maybe he's just surprising me, taking me on holiday to see if I like the country." I didn't want to say so but her naivety was frustrating.

"Talk to him tonight, see what he has to say. If I'm wrong I'm sorry but I don't think I am." I *knew* I wasn't wrong.

Chapter 3

Gary came back into the house with a parcel in his hands. He began speaking as Mum admired her early birthday present, a pair of black high heels which she'd bought herself.

"Lynette wouldn't open the door to me," Gary said.

"What do you mean?" I asked.

"I knocked on their door and waited a while but nobody answered. I knew someone was in there. I could hear them moving about in the hall. They must have heard me. I was about to leave when Lynette opened the front window. She looked terrified, but she knows who I am, I've spoken to her often enough. I asked her if I could collect a parcel delivered earlier. She left the room ... but the smell! Lemon disinfectant coming through the window. I had to step away - sickening. After a minute or so she returned and passed the parcel through the window. Why not just open the door? So strange ..."

"Weird." I said.

"She might have lost the keys," Mum said, busying herself with the straps on her heels.

"But why the smell?"

"Probably cleaning."

"No one uses that much, not even you," Gary said to Mum. "There was something suspicious about her." "You may have called at a bad time. There could be a hundred explanations, stop fussing!"

"I just thought it was a bit weird, that's all."

It was weird. I knew Declan was home. He'd been there all week, his car parked on the driveway. I wondered if Lynette had told him what I'd said that afternoon. If she had I was fearful for her. *Why wouldn't she open the door? Was he behind her strange actions?*

I was walking towards the stairs, someone was yelling at me. I wished they'd shut up. What right did they have to yell at me? After everything I'd done for them. I told them where to go. Then I was at the stairs, she was right behind me. What exactly did she think she could do? I was finished with her. Her hands grabbed me. Caught me unawares, shook me violently. I fell. Down and down. I felt my neck jolt against the stairs and my eyes shot open.

It was pitch black. I couldn't see a thing, hadn't a clue where I was, but could hear Mum's soft but urgent voice in my ear.

"Lorna ... you alright? Lorna?"

"What?"

"Come on Lorna, let's get you back to bed."

"Where am I?"

"You were sleepwalking."

"Sleepwalking?"

"Yes. I just saw you walk down the landing and rock at the top of the stairs."

"Seriously?" I asked in disbelief.

"I'm not making it up. At first, I thought you were going down to get a drink. Then you all but chucked yourself down the stairs."

"Wow." I'd never sleepwalked before.

"You could have killed yourself. Just go back to bed."

"Okay, goodnight. Sorry about that."

"You frightened the life out of me. Goodnight."

I went back to bed. I still couldn't believe I'd been sleepwalking. But if what Mum had said was true, that I'd nearly thrown myself down the stairs ... I shuddered, vaguely remembering my dream, of someone pushing me down the stairs. Odd.

I got home from college and went into the kitchen. Mum sat on the worktop.

"Maybe I should go and see her?" I heard her say.

"See who?" I asked.

"None of your business," Gary joked.

"Says you!"

"You carry on being cheeky and I won't tell you the latest gossip."

"What gossip?"

"Declan at number 4 has been having an affair."

"Oh?" I feigned surprise. "Who told you?"

"Paul."

"And he is *such* a reliable source." Paul was the biggest gossip on the street.

"He is actually telling the truth, for once," added Mum.

"Is Lynette okay?" I asked.

"I don't know ... not sure whether to go and see her or not. She was there for me after everything with your dad. This may be why she was being funny with you last night, Gary.

"Probably right."

The 'everything with Dad' happened three years ago. Mum was pregnant with my brother, Bobby, and Dad had been having an affair - not the first time he'd cheated on Mum. She kicked him out. Since then I've had almost nothing to do with him, and he's had even less to do with Bobby. Dad hadn't wanted another child. We reckon he'd wanted Mum to discover his affair so she'd have reason to leave him. His reputation would have taken a knock if people found out he'd left his pregnant wife. I see him, sometimes . Bobby and I are supposed to visit him during school holidays, it rarely happens. His excuse to avoid seeing us is usually 'working' abroad; who's he kidding? I couldn't care less. Mum has Gary, she's happy and he's all the 'dad' Bobby needs.

I saw that Declan's car was gone from the drive and wondered where he was and whether he'd just made empty threats. If he was going to do anything, he'd surely have tried something today while I was walking to college or back. I fell asleep worrying.

"You can't kick me out of my own house!" he said, furiously.
"You're leaving anyway," Lynette spat out.
"It's my house. I pay the mortgage. I pay the bills. I paid for the food in the fridge."
"I work!" She shouted.
"In a bloody charity shop! You don't even get paid."
"I enjoy it. It makes me feel useful."
"As long as you're happy, Lynette," he mocked, "whereas I'm working all hours to support you."
"Us! You work for us! I'm your wife. What's your's is mine."
"Why do you think I'm leaving? You're a fat, lazy cow and you're not sponging off my money any longer." She slapped him. Hard.
"You'll regret that." He grabbed her shoulders and pushed her against the wall. She tried shaking him off but he was too strong. "I should kill you now," he sneered. She shouted and screamed and squirmed but his grip tightened. "That little bitch spoilt all my plans. I'll kill her too."
"Is this how you threatened her?" (She meant me.)
"She told you?"
"She told me you'd threatened her. She told me you weren't taking me to Singapore."
"Of course I'm not taking you!"
"Why pretend you were?"

9

"To put you off my trail. It was fun. You're so gullible. How you sucked in my story of the holiday. How excited you were, your face when you saw the photos of the apartment. My apartment! And you'll never set one foot in it. You'll never set one foot in Singapore. The tickets aren't for me and you. They're for me and Nicola."

"If you weren't happy why didn't you leave me months ago, years ago?"

"And let you have the house? Have you force me to sell my car and give you half my savings? You're not getting another penny from me."

"I've never asked for anything from you."

"You expect it," he spat.

"Get out!" She screamed in his face. He backed away.

"I'm going. I can't stand the sight of your face and your body any longer. You disgust me. You don't even try and look nice anymore. You may not mind looking like an ugly whore, but I do. You embarrass me."

"I hate you!" She followed behind him. At the top of the stairs she grabbed him and shook him violently. Then she pushed him. He fell. Down and down.

"Lorna! Lorna!" Someone was shaking me. I felt cold hands.

"Mummy, Mummy, Lorna's gone mad," Bobby whimpered.

"That happened a long time ago," I said in a daze.

"Mummy, Lorna's scaring me. What's wrong with Lorna, Mummy?" Bobby was trembling and crying, clutching tightly onto Mum.

"What happened?" I asked.

"You were yelling."

"I don't remember a thing." I still hadn't woken up properly and the dream was already fading.

"You could've woken the dead."

"Sorry."

"Are you okay, Lorna?" Mum looked concerned.

"Yeah." She looked long and hard at me. Neither of us spoke.

"Back to bed Bobby, Lorna's okay now."

"Can I have another bedtime story?"

"It's two o'clock in the morning, son." Bobby looked at her, his expression blank, wondering what the time had to do with a story.

"Pleeeeease."

"No. It's the middle of the night."

"But Mummy, Lorna woke me up."

"I said no." She picked him up off my bed and carried him back to his room. He started crying when she left him. I laid in the dark listening.

His crying became hiccups but he eventually fell asleep. I took much longer.

Friday. Last day of term before a week-long break. I picked Bobby up at nursery straight from college. My thought was that Declan surely wouldn't bother me if I was with my kid brother. Despite trying to convince myself otherwise, maybe I was a bit afraid of him. I kept watch for a black Jaguar the whole walk home; any black car stopped my heart for a millisecond.

"How many sleeps until we see Dad?" asked Bobby.

"Three."

"Yay! Do you think he'll play monsters with me, like Gary does?"

"Maybe." I doubted Dad would play anything with Bobby. He always made excuses. It'd be a wonder if Bobby recognised his dad anyway. God knows why he was so excited about seeing him. It was all he'd been going on about for days, driving Mum and Gary mad. They both disliked my dad, but a three year old doesn't know when to keep its mouth shut.

"Lorna, Bobby, is that you?" Mum yelled from the kitchen as I closed the front door.

"Yes, Mum."

"Mummyyyyyyyyyyy." Bobby yelled as he ran into the kitchen.

"Bobby, be careful. Go upstairs and put your book bag away." I turned to go upstairs but Mum called me back.

"Lorna, can I have a word?"

"Yep." She was being conspiratorial so I was instantly curious.

"Up you go Bobby. Come, sit here Lorna." I sat down at the table, slightly anxious.

"Lorna, has anything happened at college?"

"Nope, why?"

"Anything to do with a boy?"

"No!" *Why do mums have to be so nosy?*

"Work isn't too stressful is it?"

"No Mum, I'm fine."

"I was reading up about sleepwalking and sleep problems. Stress can be a trigger. Are you sure nothing is up?"

"I'm sure." Should I tell her about Declan? (Maybe, but she'd only worry.) His car had gone, so had he, and he was leaving for Singapore the next day. There was nothing anyone could do now. Once he was out of the country I'd be fine. Admittedly, I'd been thinking about him a lot, but I doubted that was the reason for my sleepwalking and yelling. I didn't feel that stressed.

"You're not lying to me? You can talk to me about anything, you know." She couldn't possibly know about *him*.

"I know Mum, but I'm fine."

"Good. I've got something to tell you."

"O ... kay?" *Now I was worrying.*

"Gary and I have been together almost two years now. And we're engaged."

"Yes?"

"I found out something last week."

"Yes?"

"I'm pregnant!"

"Mum, that's brilliant!" I jumped up and gave her big a hug.

"Are you sure it's okay?" She sounded relieved.

"Yes, of course it's okay. It's fantastic. Congratulations. How many weeks along are you?"

"Ten." I went and congratulated Gary and called Bobby back downstairs.

"I'm not having another sister," he told Mum, "they're boring and stupid." Cheers Bobby! We went out for tea to celebrate. Gary couldn't stop grinning. His first child. I was happy for them. We passed number 4 on the walk home.

"He said he was going to leave you." A tall woman with blonde hair, perfectly styled in loose curls, shouted at Lynette on her doorstep. She wore a short black dress and fur coat. Even in the dark I could see the six inch heels, the fake tan and the make-up.

"He has." Lynette replied sharply.

"Then where is he?" The woman shrieked.

"In hell for all I care."

"Don't lie!" The woman's voice now hysterical. "I haven't seen or heard from him since Wednesday. You know where he is."

"Not only do I not know where he is, I don't care where he is. In Singapore I hope. Now, get off my property."

"He wouldn't have gone to Singapore without me."

"I wouldn't blame him if he had."

"What's that supposed to mean?"

"That you're a high maintenance tart who'll drain his bank account in months."

"I'm a sophisticated woman. I take pride in my appearance, unlike some who dress in charity's finest. And I'll have you know I work for all my money."

"As a prostitute." Lynette slammed her door shut. The woman stood, appalled and in shock.

"What are you looking at?" The woman bellowed when she noticed us looking on. We just walked silently on to our door.

"If that's his mistress, he hasn't done too badly." Gary joked once we were inside. Mum gave him 'the look'.

"She's a tarted up monster," she said.

"I feel sorry for the bloke when she finds him."

"I don't."

I got a text that night from Dad, saying he was working so couldn't look after us. Mum was furious, she'd booked a few days away with Gary.

"I mean, who does he think he is? Giving us two days' notice. Not even a phone call. What if your phone was turned off Lorna? What would we have done then? The swine. Do you think I like asking him to have you? If it was up to me neither of you would have any contact with him. But he's your dad so I can't stop you. All I asked was for one week. I haven't been away anywhere in three years." Mum raged. "I mean, what are we going to do now? Everything's paid for. We might get a bit of the money back but we've lost most of it in deposits. For crying out loud! Your father Lorna, just wait until I see him."

"Liz, calm down, come on. You shouldn't be stressing," Gary said.

"How can I not? He's just lost us hundreds of pounds. We can't afford to throw away that sort of money, not with a baby on the way. Anyway, the money doesn't matter, it's the principle. The number of times he's let you and Bobby down ... it's not right. I mean to say, he's only seen his son, what ... five times in his life ... probably less." She paced up and down, her voice rising with every word.

"Mum, I don't mind, really. I wasn't expecting anything anyway. And Bobby's better off without him." I tried to placate her.

"You see what I mean? Bobby's better off without him. What kind of father is that? He doesn't deserve you Lorna, or Bobby. Fair enough if you were two naughty brats, but you're not. You're good kids and deserve better. You hear me Lorna, you deserve better." Mum was really fired up. Gary sat wordless on the sofa.

"Mum, stop getting yourself worked up. He's not worth it." But, oblivious to my voice she carried on.

"Work? Yeah right. He'll be off with his next fancy tart in some nightclub. I mean, how old is he? Forty-odd. You'd think he'd have stopped clubbing and getting plastered twenty years ago. But no, not your father. He's still the immature, lazy teen he was all those years ago. The number of times he left us to go away to *work*, when, really, he was hitting on any grubby slapper he could lay his hands on. Three years ago he left. And bloody good riddance ... happiest day of my life, I'm telling you. Yet, some way or another he still manages to control me. This time he's crossed the line. He's never letting you kids down again. Never." Tears streamed down her face. I hated seeing her like this. And I hated Dad for doing this to her. All the bloody time. Gary walked Mum upstairs. Two minutes later I heard him running her bath. Bless him.

Sometimes I feel sorry for Gary, especially when Dad pulls a stunt like this. He'll say it doesn't matter but I can tell he's frustrated. It's not fair on him. I mean, he's worked hard for this holiday with Mum and money's tight right now, especially with a new baby coming. At times like this Gary keeps his distance. He doesn't like interfering in 'family matters' but they always involve him because now he's part of the family, and a better dad to Bobby. Bobby - he was another problem. What was I going to say to him? I don't 'hate' my dad but I hate him for doing this all the time. Personally, it didn't bother me but everyone else is always left disappointed and upset, and that hurt.

About ten minutes later Gary came down and sat opposite me. Even after all the shouting his friendly face never altered. He smiled at me, dimples in his chubby cheeks. Gary's not fat, just a bit on the chubby side. His six-foot-something height balances out his weight so he looks average. His thinning brown hair a tad too long hung limply from his face. He wore an old dark green jumper and jeans that had seen better days. The slight scruffiness suited him perfectly. His kindly nature made up for anything his appearance lacked. Mum loved him for who he was, not what he looked like, which she says was her downfall when falling for my father. She's so much happier now with Gary.

"She's calmed down now," he said. "I went to check on Bobby, he was

14

crying. I told him that his mum was just upset about something, nothing to worry about. I didn't want to tell him his dad had let him down again."

"I'll go up now and tell him." I stood up. Gary smiled and I left the room. I walked upstairs, telling myself I had to phone my dad but worrying I wouldn't be strong enough to stand up to him. I could picture him laughing, mocking me, insulting Mum and Gary. I stood outside Bobby's door in dread. It always came down to this, me feeling guilty because of my dad. I was the one who had to explain to a three year old why his dad didn't want to see him. I began hating my father that little bit more.

Standing outside Bobby's door I knew what the night would bring. In the end it was worse than I'd imagined. I took a deep breath and went in. He stared up at me, eyes puffy, red and accusing, like it was all my fault that Mum was angry and upset.

"Hey, come on! A big brave boy like you doesn't cry." He didn't reply so I climbed into his bed and snuggled up to him. He pushed me away. I lay my head on the pillow and looked at him. He turned to the wall so all I saw was a great mop of brown hair. I didn't know how to break it to him. He'd been so looking forward to seeing his dad. I think he'd imagined this great 'dad' in his head but I doubted he'd remember what he looked like.

"Bobby." I ran my fingers through his hair. "Next week, Dad's going away, so he won't be able to look after us. We have to stay here." I whispered, not wanting the words to come out.

"No!" He screamed so loud it almost deafened me. He threw the bed covers off and sprang up, his face bright red. "No! You promised Lorna! You promised! You promised! You promised!" Stamping his feet on the mattress and shaking his tiny fists. I sat up to avoid being trodden on.

"I know I did Bobby. And I'm really, really sorry. But Dad has to go to work. He won't be able to see us Bobby." *I hadn't promised anything. I wouldn't have been that stupid.*

"Liar! Daddy will see me. He said so. He will see me. You're a liar Lorna. A nasty stupid liar!" He yelled so loud his voice cracked and he started coughing violently. I was surprisingly hurt by his words but it I couldn't really blame him, and he was breaking my heart.

"I'm sorry Bobby. So sorry. Really, really, really sorry." I tried hugging him.

"No! No! No! No! No!" He screamed, lashing out, hitting and kicking, his little face all screwed up in rage. Beating me with his small but powerful fists I stayed until I could take it no more. I tried fending him off but he was having none of it. I pushed him away when his hands began clawing at my face. He fell back down on his bed squealing, as though I'd hurt him. I knew I hadn't.

"I hate you!" He screamed as I walked away. About to leave the room I felt something hit my back. It was jimmy jammy, his little ragdoll. I closed his door, went to my room and collapsed onto my bed. Mum's muffled sobs from the bathroom next door were just audible above Bobby's screeching and yelling. The house reverberated with banging sounds coming from Bobby's room. His toys were bouncing off the walls, bookcases and drawers were being overturned, Bobby jumping up and down on the floor. I wanted to yell at him to stop but I felt more sorry for him than angry. The front door opened and closed. A car door slammed. An engine revved. Headlights shone through the curtains. Slowly all grew silent. When Gary came in he asked Mum and I to come downstairs.

"I've been to my Mum's and she's happy to have Lorna and Bobby next week, so we can still go away, Liz." Then he looked at me. "Lorna, what's happened to your face?"

"Bobby scratched me."

"Bobby did that?" Mum looked horrified. To be honest, I hadn't even looked at my face but it was stinging, and he had hurt me.

"Yeah."

"I'll be having words with him in the morning."

"He was upset." I said.

"No difference. He's not a baby anymore. He can't go on hurting people. I should send him packing to his Dad's whether Andrew likes it or not ... see if he can sort out his son. His tantrums are worsening. And your mum is definitely not looking after him if he's playing up like that."

"My Mum isn't a frail old woman. She's perfectly capable of looking after a child. Lorna will be there anyway."

"Fine. But I'm not happy."

"He's not ruining our break."

"He can do whatever the hell he likes. He always does."

"Liz, please, forget about him for now."

"Hello. Andrew speaking." Dad in his 'phone voice'.

"Hi Dad, it's Lorna."

"Oh … you alright?"

"Yeah, thanks. You?"

"Yes, how's school?" *I was at college.*

"Alright, same as usual. How's work?" Same old small talk.

"You know, busy."

"Yeah, where are you off to next week?"

"I'm at home until Thursday but I'll be working late every night. Flying to Germany early Friday morning."

"Why can't Bobby and I stay until Thursday?" I asked.

"I'm working and I can't look after Bobby."

"I can look after him."

"No. Bobby will get bored and play up."

"You said you'd see us for the week."

"Plans change."

"Mum's already booked her holiday … you knew that."

"Work is more important than a holiday. She should have booked to take you two with her."

"You're always going on holiday without us. She's never been on holiday without me or Bobby."

"I can hear your mum's words there. I knew she'd poison your mind. Remember, it's your mum who wanted a divorce. She was the one who split up the family."

"And I don't blame her! She split up with you not us. She's never stopped you from seeing us."

"Lorna. Be quiet. You don't know what you're talking about. I'm not having your mum telling you I'm a terrible father. I work and I provide for you, and Lorna … if you want to see me next week then you can. Never let your mum tell you I don't want to see you because I do. You're always welcome at my house. I'll pick you up Sunday if you want?"

"What about Bobby?" I didn't even know where he lived now. His last excuse for not seeing us was that he was moving house so he was too busy.

"What have I just told you? I don't have time to look after Bobby and that's final. I'll see you Sunday. Bye."

"Bye." He hung up. I was seething.

Chapter 4

Sunday afternoon. I was sitting in Gary's mum's living room. Mum and Gary had already left for the hotel. I hadn't told Mum the whole conversation with Dad, only that I was going to see him and he was working so couldn't look after Bobby. I had promised I'd talk to Dad about Bobby. It was after five o'clock when he turned up, despite having arranged for noon. He'd doubtless have an excuse and that it wasn't his fault. He arrived in an expensive black Mercedes. I could tell by the number plate it was new. Bobby was happily playing with his cars. He'd been to 'soft play'. He should have been there when Dad collected me. Nanna asked, "Bobby, do you want to get your bike out the shed and we'll go for a ride?" It was an excuse to get him out the way so he wouldn't see his Dad. I'd told him I'd be staying with friends. Bobby stood up, about to run to the back door when Dad beeped his car horn. Bobby looked outside. Heart in my mouth I prayed he wouldn't recognise his father.

"Dad!"

I'd love to know how he'd recognised the man behind the wheel, but he had. He screamed and shot out the door faster than I could stop him. He was struggling to open the garden gate as I wrapped my arms around his waist, lifted him up and turned him around. He stared at me, perplexed. I knelt down and looked him in the eye. Nanna stood at the front door, knowing what was coming, what she'd have to deal with when I left.

"Bobby, I have to go with Dad. You will have to stay with Nanna this time. Is that alright?" My heart sank as his excited face quickly faded.

"I want to go with Dad." His lip began to quiver, he was going to cry.

"I know you do and next time you will. But this time it's just me."

"Why can't I go?" His voice was thick, his face all screwed up and turning pink, then red.

"I need to speak to Dad because he hasn't been very nice."

"I can speak to Dad." Tears brimmed in his eyes.

"No Bobby, not right now. I'm sorry. Dad is very busy this week but I'm going to speak to him and make him see us more."

"Why can't he see me now?" He tried dodging around me to open the gate. I took his small hand and managed to prise it free of the gate.

"I don't know. But he can't right now, but you will see him soon." How could I tell him his dad didn't want to see him?

"Please let me see Dad, Lorna." I stood up, resenting the fact that he thought it was my fault. I eased open the gate behind me and edged out.

"I'll be good ..."

"I know you will. But this week you need to be good for Nanna." He tried following me out the gate but I closed it before he could push past. "I will not be good for Nanna. I won't, I won't!" He screamed, shaking the bars of the gate and stamping his feet. I walked to the car and opened the passenger door, unable to bear his crying anymore. Dad wore a smart black suit, silver cufflinks and a neat blue tie knotted crisply at his neck. Even his top collar button was fastened and he was clean-shaven. His short black hair had recently been trimmed and his grey patches dyed black. He looked a different person. His appearance had always been his priority, but here he was dressed in clothes more suited to a formal dinner, not travelling. It was all too much, dressed in arrogance to parade his wealth. He turned to look at me, his face emotionless.

"Get your bag and get in the car." His voice was stern.

"Won't you just speak to Bobby for a minute, please?"

"I don't have time to speak to him, and I can't be doing with a screaming toddler."

"Just for one minute?"

"I'll not tell you again, get your bag and get in the car." There was no point arguing any further so I got back out the car to get my bag. Nanna stood at the gate, my bag in her hand. Bobby was still shouting, his red face a snotty, teary mess. Poor kid.

"Bobby, Dad's really busy at the moment so he can't speak to you today. But another time you can go and see him." I said goodbye to Nanna and walked back to the car. I looked back from the passenger seat and saw Bobby open the gate and run out onto the street before Nanna could stop him.

"Dad." I heard him shout. Dad started the engine. "Dad. Dad. Dad." He was running towards the car as fast as his little legs could carry him. Dad didn't so much as look behind. He drove away down the street. I could hear Bobby's high-pitched wail of hopelessness as we turned the corner. Then he was gone. I have never hated my Dad more.

"You knew Bobby wasn't coming so why upset him like that?" I couldn't believe it, but then what had I expected from him?

"If you'd come when you said you would Bobby wouldn't have been there. And if you hadn't beeped your horn Bobby wouldn't have seen you." I was furious and heartbroken for Bobby.

"So, it's my fault your brother is throwing a tantrum?"

"Your son! And yes, it is." I shouldn't be provoking him, it wouldn't solve anything but I was past caring. He no longer scared me; I'd met meaner men.

"My fault?" Dad laughed. "I'm your father Lorna ... your cheek has got to stop."

"But you never see him."

"I talk to him over the phone."

"But you never see him."

"I'm too busy to be trailing up and down the country every other weekend to see him. He has to learn that."

"I know, but you haven't seen him in months."

"I've just bought a new house. It's been too hectic to have him running around. Besides, I don't have any toys for him, there's nothing for him to do, and there isn't a park round the corner for him to play in. He'll be bored."

"Buy some toys. You're just making excuses."

"Now listen to me young lady. I work and provide for you two which is a damn sight more than some dads. I brought you up until you were in your teens, so don't question my parenting." It's the lack of parenting I was fussed about, but I kept my mouth shut. *Bobby is better off without him. But how could I tell him that?*

Dad made small talk that was going nowhere. He turned on the radio. We sat in silence most of the way. I hadn't seen him for months but I had nothing to say. A couple of hours' driving later we pulled into a motorway service station. He bought me a hot chocolate and a magazine - subtle peace offering. He'd never apologise verbally ... far too stubborn.

"I don't want to argue with you Lorna."

"You can't choose one child over another."

"I'm not doing that. I just don't know how to look after a toddler. Your mum is good at that stuff. I barely know Bobby. I wouldn't know how to deal with him."

"He's not some wild animal. He's your son. You think Mum knows how to deal with him all the time? Do you see the scratch next to my eye?" He nodded. "That was from dealing with one of Bobby's tantrums when I had to tell him you couldn't see him this week." He was looking over my shoulder, his face expressionless. He sipped at his coffee. My scratches had mostly faded but a couple of red abrasions were still visible from where Bobby had broken the skin.

"You've really grown up since I last saw you."

"How grown up will Bobby have to be before you see him? Six? Ten? Eighteen?"

"I can't believe I'm having this conversation with my little girl. I'll see Bobby when I have time to look after him."

"Make time."

"It's not as easy as that. I have work commitments."

"Mum works. So does Gary. I work, and go to college yet each of us makes time to look after him."

"My work is more demanding. I travel all over the world. I'm nearly always on call. It's not practical for me to see you both as often as you'd like." *He thinks I want to see him*? But of course, his work is far more important than Mum's or Gary's.

"Seeing him at all would be a start." I mumbled into my hot chocolate.

"Just leave it Lorna. I'll see him when I can and there's nothing more I can say."

"If it isn't soon he'll forget you. He's already asked Gary to be his dad." I regretted the words instantly, but they'd needed saying. He didn't look at me, and swigged back his coffee. He forcefully put down his empty cardboard cup onto the table; that's how I knew my words had hit home. He stood up and walked out, back to the car. I followed.

He drove on for another couple of hours, no word passing between us until we reached his house. It was dark and I wasn't really concentrating on where we were going. We turned off the motorway and headed down country roads and through small villages. He pulled into a narrow lane, lined with trees. No street lamps. It didn't even look like a road. He turned left and the headlights lit up a pair of enormous black iron gates. He punched in a code on a security panel. They opened.

"Where are we?" I asked.

"Home." He replied, rather smug.

"This is *your* house?" I was taken aback.

"It's your house too, Lorna." Apart from the huge building in front of me I couldn't see much in the dark.

"I built it. Well, not me personally, but I had it built. That's why I've been busy the past few months. I've been renting a flat while this place was being built. It's all finished now, though." He was smiling. He pulled up beside the garage to the right of the house, an outside light automatically turning on. He opened his door. I was gazing out over the dark fields unable make out anything but trees.

"What the ..." Dad exclaimed, jumping out the car. I also got out.

"Why are you here?" A young woman approached him; a pregnant young woman.

"I need to see you."

"How did you get through the gates?"

"I walked through the trees at the back."

"That woodland is hundreds of metres thick."

She shrugged. "I needed to see you."

"Well, now you've seen me. You can go." His anger was obvious.

"I'm not leaving. You got me into this mess."

"Lorna, get inside ... now." He turned and threw me his bundle of keys. I caught them but didn't move.

"Lorna? That's a new one. Never heard of her before." She looked me up and down in a disgusted manner.

"Lorna, inside *now*." I stepped away from the car and began walking towards the house, passing the woman. She wore a thick, green coat - hood up. I could see how thin she was with long skinny fingers and gaunt face. Her jeans were baggy, her trainers scruffy. But her stomach was huge by comparison, bulging out from beneath her coat.

"Don't you think she's a bit young, Andrew? Even by your standards." I stopped a couple of metres from the door. She intrigued me.

"Lorna is my daughter. Now, get off my land or I'll remove you myself."

"You wouldn't dare."

"It's my property. I do what I like."

"I'm having your baby. A little more respect, please."

"Respect? I found you in a *strip club* and you want respect?" He whispered the two damning words but I heard them.

"You've no right to judge me. I'm having your child, and thanks to you I have nowhere else to go."

"Do you really think I'm that gullible? I bet you're telling the same story to several other men."

"The baby is yours!"

"And how am I supposed to believe you?"

"Just because you sleep with someone different every week doesn't mean we all do."

"Lorna. I told you to get inside." I didn't move.

"You're a lap dancer. You sleep with someone different every night." She slapped him. Hard.

"I'm a dancer, not a prostitute!"

"Lorna. Inside!" He bellowed. I unlocked the door and stood in the doorway. "I will not touch a woman, especially not a pregnant one, but hit me again and I'll phone the police. Now, get off my property!"

"I have nowhere to go."

"You should have thought of that before getting knocked up."

"Do you think I wanted to come here? Do you think I want to grovel for your help? I have no choice. I have no money, nowhere to live and it's your fault. You got me pregnant, and now I can't work. The club sacked me, won't give me maternity pay, and the boss laughed when I threatened legal action. I couldn't afford the rent on my flat so my landlord kicked me out. I can't go to any family. I'm penniless and I don't know what to do. I don't want your charity. Do you think I want is, lowering myself in this way? You're the father of this child. You have a responsibility to support me."

"There's nothing I can do. I don't owe you anything. If I let you into my house you'll steal the first thing you get your hands on."

"I'm not a criminal. When the baby is born I'll prove it's yours."

"So, come back when the baby is born. I'll do a stupid test but until then I don't want to see you."

"What am I supposed to do until then?"

"Get a taxi away from here." Dad flipped open his wallet and gave her a twenty pound note. "Surely social welfare will have to help you." He turned, marched towards me and on through the door. I followed. He turned on the light and immediately locked the door.

"I thought I told you to wait inside?" Oddly, he didn't seem annoyed with me.

"Do I have other brothers and sisters I don't know about?"

"None! And there won't be any either because that baby is not mine."

"Did you sleep with her?" I couldn't believe I'd asked that. I felt myself blushing. He just looked at me, embarrassed. He didn't need to speak and I knew the answer.

"So, it could be yours then."

"It's not. It just isn't. I don't want to be questioned anymore tonight. I need a drink. I'll be in my office so please don't disturb me. I need time to think and I'm not having another argument. My bedroom is straight up the stairs on the right, you can have any of the others." He walked through the door straight ahead and left me alone in his massive unfamiliar house.

The stairs in front of me were huge, about five times the width of a normal staircase, carpeted in red and branching off in opposite directions at the first floor. I was contemplating going up but instead turned back to where he'd left his keys at the front entrance. My bag was still in the back of his car … and he'd said he didn't want disturbing. I unlocked the door and took the car keys. They jangled as I picked them up and my muscles tensed, anticipating him coming back. I took a deep breath and slowly pushed down on the handle. The door opened and I stepped out, gently closing it behind me, trying not to make a sound.

"Hello?" I spoke into the dark emptiness, wondering where she was. No answer. I walked towards the car. "Anyone there?"

"Who's that?"

"It's Lorna. Andrew's daughter."

"What do you want?" I didn't think she was being purposely hostile.

"I figured you'd still be out here." What, exactly, *did* I want? She walked round the car towards me.

"I don't have anywhere else to go. Courtesy of your father."

"There must be somewhere." She looked at me as if I was clueless.

"It took me hours to walk here. I've sat in the cold for hours more, not knowing when Andrew would turn up. Do you think I'd do that if there was anywhere else?" I shook my head. "It's dark and I'm miles away from anywhere ... what am I going to do?" She was biting her bottom lip.

"I'll help you," I said, determinedly.

"You, daughter of his bloody lordship, are going to help me?" She laughed.

"Yeah."

"Can you give me money?"

"I don't have any." The look on her face said she didn't believe me.

"You don't trust me."

"I don't know you."

"Well I'm sorry Lorna. I don't think you can help me very much at the moment."

"I will, but is the baby definitely Dad's?"

"I'm not a slapper! You know what? Just go back inside to your dad. I don't need you or your dad. I've managed this far by myself." She turned and started walking away.

"Wait. When did you tell him about the baby?" She hesitated then turned back to face me.

"Months ago. I used to kip at his flat a couple of nights when he was home. I told him one morning, almost as soon as I knew myself. I don't know what I expected. But I learnt all men are the same - useless scumbags. He accused me of cheating and kicked me out. I don't know how he dared, I mean it wasn't serious between us but he knew I hadn't been with anyone since ... since I moved away." She hesitated at the end of her sentence, seemingly drifting off to another world.

"Moved away?"

"I grew up hundreds of miles from here ... needed a fresh start. Came up here about a year ago. Someone I knew had a contact - she got me the job. I wasn't planning on staying at the club but it was money until I found something better."

"Can't you go back to where you lived before?"

"No." She answered so abruptly I knew not to ask anymore.

"Have you seen Dad since then?"

"He didn't answer my calls or texts. I tried the flat but he was never there. When my bump started showing and I'd lost the job I went back to his flat. New people had moved in and they gave me his new address here. The house wasn't finished when I came round so I spoke to the developers. They told me when Andrew would be home so I came back. Your dad made his feelings perfectly clear when he saw me. I haven't been back until today."

"Are you sure there's nowhere else for you to go?"

"I wouldn't be here if there was."

"What about the person who got you your job?"

"No chance."

"Family? Parents?" She looked furious at that suggestion.

"Don't you think I've tried? They just reminded me why I'd left in the first place. I have this bag on my back and that's all."

"I can't let you stay out here tonight."

"I have nowhere to go."

"I'm sure the house has enough bedrooms."

"The house? This house?" she asked, astonished.

"Yep." *What was I doing?*

"No way. He'd kill me, and then you!"

"Which is why he'll never find out."

"And how do you propose hiding a pregnant woman?"

"It's a big house. He said he's in the study ... doesn't want disturbing. It's just for one night. First thing in the morning we'll think of something else."

"But what if he does find me?"

"I'll make sure he doesn't. You can't stay out here. It's warm inside. There's food and a bed."

"Why are you doing this?"

"I'm doing it for my brother or sister." She nodded. I grabbed my bag from the car and we both went back to the house.

"What's your name?" It had just occurred to me I didn't know her name.

"Kate."

I got to the door and strained my eyes to see through the clouded glass. The hallway light was still on but I couldn't see Dad. I opened the door.

"Come on ..." I mumbled.

"I don't think this is a good idea," she whispered.

"You got a better one?" No answer. I stepped inside.

"It's safe. Go up the stairs as quickly as possible. I'll be right behind you." She crept inside. I followed, closed the door carefully behind me and locked it.

I took the stairway branching left and opened a door to my right. (Kate was behind me. I could tell the stairs weren't easy for her.) It opened into a huge bathroom ... white marble and a Jacuzzi. (I'd admire them later.) I climbed a couple more steps twisting left onto a landing with two doors. I took the first right, into a bedroom ... flicked on a light. The floorboards were real oak and there stood a king size bed. There were built-in wardrobes with floor-to-ceiling mirrors. Other than that, the room was bare. Another door to the back left of the room opened into an en-suite, quite a big one, with a door on the other side of it leading into another room almost identical to the one I'd just been in. I went through that door, guessing it would be the room behind the door at the end of the corridor. I dropped my bag on the floor of the first bedroom and Kate flopped back onto the bed, sighing.

"It's been months since I slept on a nice bed. I don't want to move."

"I'll go down and get some food. You rest, but if you hear Dad hide in the wardrobe or something."

"I will do. Thanks." I felt slightly sick, knowing I'd invited a stranger into my dad's house. I knew I was being too trusting and could be making a huge mistake, but my conscience would be worse off had I done nothing. I passed the bathroom and carried on down the stairs. I opened a door to the left of the one Dad had gone through. A plasma screen TV hung on the wall and there was a large red leather suite opposite. An electric fire was built into the wall and a large archway led into the dining room. I walked through the archway and the dining room curved around into a huge open plan kitchen. The floor was tiled black, the kitchen by contrast a sleek white. Clean and modern, looking as though it had never been used. I opened the large American style fridge - all but empty. The cupboards were slightly more promising. I found some pasta and a jar of tomato sauce. Finding a pan I placed it on a gleaming hob that also looked unused. The ceiling rose to about six metres high and the back wall of the kitchen and dining room was

27

solid glass. In the dark I couldn't see out as the glass just showed a darker reflection of the house, but I knew it would look spectacular in the morning. I now knew the door Dad had walked through led to the kitchen, but another door to the right of the kitchen had a coded lock on it. I guessed that to be his study. If he had heard me clattering about in the kitchen he didn't come out to investigate. I filled a large bowl with pasta and sauce, took a fork and spoon and went back upstairs. If Dad saw two bowls he'd be suspicious. Kate sat on the bed, her bag open beside her.

"That en-suite is bigger than my old bedroom," she said.

"You should see the kitchen. I brought food." She took the bowl and ate a mouthful.

"I can't remember when last I had a warm meal. I haven't been able to afford any gas or electric on the meter for ages." I didn't really know what to say so I ate the pasta. A little teddy peeked out of her bag.

"Is that for the baby?" I asked. She picked up the teddy and held it in her palm.

"Yeah." It seemed to sadden her. She pulled out a blanket and a couple of babygros. "It's all I've got for the baby."

"Dad will have to provide for the baby. Do you know if it's a boy or a girl?" I tried sounding positive.

"No."

"It'll be a nice surprise."

"Yeah, something like that." *Something was wrong.*

"When's the baby due?" I guessed it was soon.

"I don't know. A couple of weeks, less maybe or more."

"Hasn't the hospital told you?" I was confused. She shifted her body uncomfortably.

"I haven't been to the hospital."

"What! Why?"

"They'll realise I can't support the baby and take it from me when it's born."

"They won't do that. You can't not go to the hospital. You need to make sure the baby's healthy, that you're healthy."

"I have no house, no money. Have you seen the state of me? They'll never let me keep my baby."

"You've got me now. And my dad, once he knows the baby is his."

"What're you going to do?"

"I'm going to take you to the council tomorrow. They have to help you find accommodation."

"They'll phone social services. They won't let me keep the baby. I'm not living in a hostel."

"It will be somewhere to live, for a couple of weeks. I'll tell them Dad will support you. Dad can help pay for somewhere for you and the baby to live. He has to."

"They'll say I'm unfit to look after a baby."

"What other option do you have? You can't exactly stay here. They'll find you somewhere to live."

"I won't let them take my baby off me."

"They won't. I'll be with you and once they know Dad's the father, they'll know he can provide for you both. They won't take the baby."

She didn't reply.

"Please don't take offence," I started in a hushed voice, "and I will still help you either way … but is the baby definitely my dad's?" I felt rude, stuck up and judgemental by asking but I needed to know. Annoyance flashed across her face for a moment but then her face softened.

"Yes. 100%, I promise. I'm not lying." Her voice was assuring. "God knows why you'd believe me. I'm an absolute mess. Christ, I'm probably not much older than you and I've slept with your dad. How sick is that?" I couldn't tell how old she was but she didn't look much older than twenty.

"I'm more disgusted with him but that doesn't matter. Will you let me help you tomorrow?"

"I guess I don't have a choice." But she looked worried. Me too, but I was more concerned for my little brother or sister.

I took the bowl downstairs to wash up. Dad came out of his study while I was drying the dishes.

"I'm glad you found something to eat. I'll try and go shopping tomorrow night."

"I had some pasta." I carried on drying, without looking at him. He walked over to me and put the pots away.

"What bedroom are you in?"

"The one up the stairs on the left."

"Do you like the house?"

"Yeah. It looks great."

"Good. I like having you here." I nodded, unsure of what to say. He put his hand in a pocket, took out a key and passed it to me. "It's for you. I'll be at work tomorrow but you can go wherever you want. There's a bus stop at the end of the lane. You'll see it. I think a bus comes at quarter to the hour that will take you into town."

"Thanks."

"The code for the gate is 5286. There's a button in the hallway near the door to open it from the inside."

"Okay."

"Lorna, don't judge me for what happened earlier. I'll sort it somehow. It's not what it looks like. I can explain another night. It's nothing like what happened with your mum, I promise. I'm off to bed now."

"Okay. I'll be up in my room."

"Good night." He gave me a hug and his chin rested on my head. "I love you."

"Good night." I hugged him back for a second then pulled away. He'd noticed the lack of 'love you too' and maybe that hurt him slightly. But I was far from prepared to say it for his benefit. We walked up to bed. I took the steps to the left, he went straight ahead onto the first floor landing. I opened the door to my room and held my finger to my lips so Kate wouldn't speak.

"Dad's going to bed but he might be walking around for a bit." I shut the door.

"Did he say anything about me?" Kate asked

"Only to ask that I don't judge him and he'll 'sort it out'."

"What does that mean?"

"I don't know but he has no idea you're here so we're okay for tonight. Do you want a bath?"

"Yes, please." I ran the bath for her and lay on the bed, browsing the web on my phone while she soaked. When she walked back into the bedroom she had a towel wrapped around her, but her shoulders were bare and painfully thin. Her collar bone almost broken through her skin and arms like twigs ... she looked anorexic. Her bump was huge compared to the rest of her, but I still had worries about the baby. It was obvious she hadn't been eating properly. Her wet hair hung down to her shoulders, thin and damaged. At the roots the hair colour was a dirty blonde changing to a deep auburn at the tips.

"I've just been looking on the internet and there's a Citizens Advice Bureau in town, we can go there in the morning. They'll be able to help you. The council has to provide accommodation for a pregnant woman, you've got rights."

"Will you come in with me?"

"Of course."

"Thanks." She smiled.

"Feeling any better?"

"Better than I've felt in a long time." She seemed happier. I was glad.

"Good, I'll let you get ready and have some sleep." I brushed my teeth and climbed into bed in the other room. I didn't sleep for ages, listening out for her and Dad. All went quiet long before I drifted off. I couldn't believe Kate was in the other room and Dad unaware she was in the house. I didn't know if I was doing the right thing. I couldn't trust Kate, knew nothing about her. I wanted to ask about her past, why she'd run away, but it was too personal seeing as though we'd just met. I worried for hours about hundreds of stupid things before sleep finally caught up with me.

I woke with a start. The sun was creeping beneath the curtains, lighting up the room. It was very bright and I worried I'd slept in late. I sprang out of bed, out through the en-suite and carefully opened the door to the room where Kate was sleeping … to where she should have been sleeping. The duvet had been pulled back, the bed was empty. I mentally cursed and hurried onto the landing and on down the stairs. She was walking up the steps towards me.

"Morning." She smiled.

"What're you doing?" I said in a harsh whisper.

"I was hungry." She held out her hands, an apple in each.

"What if Dad saw you? I don't want you risking your neck for an *apple*."

"*Two* apples actually." She threw one to me. "And Andrew's gone to work, I heard him leave and his car is gone."

"Good. You scared me." I carried on downstairs to get my own breakfast.

Morning sunlight seeped into the kitchen through a glass wall in front of me amplifying the length of the room. Beams of light bounced off the worktops reflecting on the white walls. The black tiled floor glistened. I stepped forward to the window; it was like looking at a painting spanning several metres upwards and quadruple that across. I gazed out over the rolling green fields stretched out for miles and miles, merging into the horizon. Woodland edged the fields to the left, the trees a mass of dark green. It felt as though I was out there, not boxed in by walls and ceiling. The view was spectacular.

The bus arrived at the time Dad had said it would, going straight into town. I used my phone to navigate our way to the Citizens Advice Bureau. Kate asked the receptionist if she could see someone. We sat in the waiting area for far too long. Kate was growing increasingly anxious. I was worried she'd walk out. When someone eventually called her she asked me to sit in with her. We sat with the advisor for over an hour. She asked Kate hundreds of questions. I wasn't sure the adviser believed me about hiding Kate in Dad's house last night but I convinced her I wouldn't be able to repeat it. After further questioning she said she was going to phone the council, and left us in the meeting room. She was gone ages. The longer she was gone the more apprehensive Kate became. Finally she returned and handed Kate an appointment card for that afternoon to see a council official. When we left the building I could see she was relieved. I bought us lunch and we went shopping for a little while. I bought a toy train for Bobby. We spent ages looking at baby clothes and I bought a couple of adorable new-born sleeping suits for Kate. We found the council offices and signed in. We suffered the same wait and the same questions as earlier. The meeting seemed to drag on for even longer by the time the legal documents were filled out and signed.

"What do you think they'll do with me?" Kate asked when the council woman walked out to talk to somebody.

"They're going to help you.

"So why has she walked out to talk to someone and not talk in front of me?"

"I don't know."

"What if she's talking to social services now, so they are warned when I have the baby?"

"That's not going to happen. She can't do that without talking to you."

I had no idea whether that was true or not. The woman returned. Kate looked eagerly at her.

"We've booked a room for you in a B&B tonight. I'll arrange another appointment for tomorrow to try and arrange longer term accommodation." She handed Kate a pack full of papers and leaflets.

"How long will I be in the B&B for?"

"Not very long I hope. I'll make further inquiries and try to find you more suitable accommodation. Please fill in those forms and read through the leaflets. If you'd like to wait downstairs I'll be with you shortly."

"That's not an answer. It might not be long before the baby comes, then what am I going to do if I'm stuck in a B&B?" Kate said when the woman had left us.

"They'll find you some other place. Come in tomorrow and see what they say."

"I hope the room isn't grotty."

"At least you've got somewhere to go. I told you they'd be able to help. They have to." The woman gave Kate a time to return the next morning and directed us to the B&B.

"I can get there myself. You need to catch the bus back home."

"Are you sure you'll be okay?"

"Yeah, it's not far."

"Do you have a phone? You can phone me when you get there."

"Yeah, but I have no credit."

I found a convenience store and bought her £10 worth of credit, ignoring her protests. We exchanged numbers.

"I'll phone you in an hour or so to make sure you're okay. Please phone me if you need something."

"I will. Thanks Lorna, for everything." We said our goodbyes and I waited for a bus to take me back to Dad's.

Walking through the gates to his house felt surreal, just like my experiences of the past day. I found it hard to believe that at the same time yesterday I'd never seen this house nor met Kate, yet I'd sneaked her in under his roof and spent all day helping a total stranger. I walked up the red carpet stairs, this time going straight ahead, struggling to believe I was alone in this massive house, probably the only person for miles around ... a strange feeling. I stepped onto a large landing with more real oak flooring. The ceiling was decorated with impressive swirls and detailed borders. Four doors led off the landing with a balcony straight ahead. I went to the glass double doors and looked out. Miles and miles of green was all that could be seen; forests surrounding the fields. I couldn't believe this was my dad's house ... amazing. On the other hand, I hated that he had all this and Kate nothing, that Mum and Gary worked all hours just to pay the bills while he swanned around this house alone. I walked through the door to my right, into his room. The bedroom was huge. The bed was up on a raised level, several steps leading up to it. The walk-in wardrobe was likely bigger than my room at home. There was an en-suite of similar size. I didn't nose around too long ... it was after all my dad's room. Another door on the landing opened into the most luxurious bathroom I'd ever seen. In the centre at the back of the room, on a raised floor, was a huge Jacuzzi positioned beneath a large circular window. Spotlights dazzled from the floor and ceiling. I had to try the Jacuzzi. I couldn't resist. It felt as though I was in some posh spa hotel in a country manor. I phoned Kate after my long, relaxing soak.

"Hey it's Lorna. Did you get to the B&B okay?"

"Yeah, I'm in my room now."

"How is it?"

"It's okay. A bit outdated and small, but it's clean and has a bed. It's somewhere to stay until I get sorted." We chatted for a bit. I was relieved she was okay. Then I put on a film on the plasma TV downstairs. It was like being at a private cinema screening. The surround sound system was awesome. Dad came home after a few hours. I went grocery shopping with him. He said he'd finished work early so I wouldn't be alone all day. Really? Together we made a curry for tea then spent the night in front of the TV. I felt guilty and hypocritical, but it was nice spending time together. He was far from forgiven and I couldn't remain angry forever.

Chapter 5

Dad and I spoke a bit more during the week. I didn't raise any awkward subjects, such as Kate or Bobby, deciding to stay silent and see what he'd do about Bobby the next time I saw him. As for Kate, there was nothing I could do or say to Dad until the baby was born as he wouldn't be convinced without a DNA test. Besides, I wasn't meant to know anything about them. I phoned Kate every day. She was still at the B&B, getting help.

The car journey home was long and tedious but with a much better atmosphere than there had been initially. Bobby ran into my arms when I walked through the door.

"Hey, Bobby! I've missed you." I ruffled his hair.

"Missed you too," he mumbled into my shoulder.

"I've got something for you." I put him down and handed him the toy train I'd bought him. He was very happy with it.

"What do you say Bobby?" asked Nanna as she walked out of the kitchen to greet me.

"Thank you."

"You're welcome."

"Do you have something else to say to Lorna?" Nanna asked.

"I made cakes for you!" He sped off into the kitchen to show me. "Bob the Builder ones." They were little fairy cakes with Bob the Builder faces on top.

"They look really yummy, Bobby."

"What are the cakes for?" Nanna asked. Bobby gazed at his feet.

"To say sorry for shouting and hitting you when you left." His voice trailed off halfway through, bless him.

"That's okay, thanks for the cakes." I gave him a cuddle.

Mum and Gary came back the next day and we went home. Once Bobby was settled and asleep Mum questioned me about Dad. I told her what had happened when he'd picked me up, and also some of the things he'd said about Bobby. She was not impressed. I didn't mention his house, or its size; just glad she didn't ask. I only told her about Bobby and that hopefully maybe the next time might be different; that what I'd said to him might have hit home. She wasn't convinced ... don't blame her.

Kate was my secret. I phoned her, as I'd promised. She was doing okay, but still stuck in the B&B. I went to draw my curtains before going to bed. The night was overcast but I could see the crescent moon peeking out from behind a cloud. I looked out over the street and my eyes wandered across to number 4. Declan's car wasn't there, a good sign. *He'll be thousands of miles away,* I told myself. I had nothing more to worry about, no more hassle from him. There were no lights on in the house. I thought of Lynette. I doubted she'd be in work but thought I might go to the shop the next day to see if anyone had heard from her. I didn't want to knock on her door.

I was walking. Purposefully. I had somewhere to go. At this moment though, I didn't know where. I was being coerced into going. Trying to think when I was commanded to walk. I could not refuse. I had to obey the command. I was not to question.
"Stop!"
I froze. My body loosened, my mind once again my own. Thinking I must have been dreaming I opened my eyes. Crisp, clean air whipped at my face. I was standing, barefoot, on cold soggy uneven ground. With deep dread I knew I definitely wasn't in my bedroom, asleep under my duvet. I had no idea where I was. It was almost pitch black, a sliver of light from a crescent moon now free of the clouds the only light visible. I stood gazing around, my eyes growing accustomed to the poor light. I made out trees, lots of trees, arched high above me in every direction. I didn't feel afraid. I wasn't scared ... not yet. I stood a while longer. Nothing happened.

Events occur in dreams. There are always people and lots of activity; never a dream where nothing happens and your only thought is of waking up. I cannot recall ever feeling cold in a dream or feeling wind on my cheeks. But I was cold and the wind was biting. I was alone and going nowhere. Harsh reality soon dawned on me. This was no dream. It was really happening. I'd woken up in the middle of the night, in the heart of a forest, with no recollection of having travelled there, and no idea where I was. Now was my time to be terrified.

I scanned the ground intensely for any clue as to where or why I was where I was. I stepped forward. My foot sank into a heap of leaves and branches, scratching my ankles. I kicked some of the branches away to find a safe spot for another step. Moving my right foot I heard an eerie crunching sound as it pressed down on the ground. It sounded much worse than snapping twigs and I felt something hard and lumpy beneath my foot - it certainly wasn't leaves or wood. I moved some branches to see - that's when I found it. Beneath the dead trampled leaves, partially concealed ... a decomposing corpse.

I sprang back, too frightened to scream. Its empty eyes stared up at me. The smell of death filled my nostrils, soured my mouth, filled my lungs. I bolted. The smell hung in the air, suffocating me. The trees, twigs and leaves scraped and scratched my soles as I scrambled barefoot, but none of that bothered me. I needed to get out of there, away from the body, the smell. It seemed to follow me. It clung to my mouth. I could taste it. My insides churned and I leant against a tree for support until my stomach settled. I then tiptoed hesitantly around the forest jumping scared stupid at a faint sound, and a branch poked my eye. Oowww! Half crouching, I darted my eyes in all directions looking for any sign of movement. As much as I hated being alone the prospect of someone else being there made my blood run cold. After a few moments I dared to move again, my eyes constantly zipping about. I prayed I wouldn't stumble across the body again. I could've been walking in circles for all I knew. The memory of bones crunching when I'd stood on the corpse stayed with me; I had to get out of the forest. My heart stopped at the slightest sound as I stared out into the darkness concealing my surroundings. Forest noises kept me on edge, their eeriness heightening my paranoia. Horror movie scenes flashed through my mind. My breathing was erratic, heartbeat inconsistent. I trembled fearfully. I stopped, breathing deeply, trying to regain control of my body, shivering uncontrollably. The night was cold and I was wearing pyjamas. Panicking didn't help, but this was the last place in the world where I should be. It was impossible not to panic. I tried to calm down but I was walking in circles so I rested against a tree to try and recover my thoughts. The wind was strong, bitterly cold. I was weakening but forced myself to start walking again. Whether for minutes or hours, time became irrelevant as I continued on for what felt like eternity, walking around endless trees: cold, tired and scared, longing for a way out of this nightmare.

I don't know exactly when it was but the solution to ending my moonlight wandering hit me as I walked into a pole. I grimaced, the surprise collision making my head ring. After a few seconds I stepped back and looked up. An arrowhead mounted on top of the thin black pole looked back down at me. I only saw it because it was a denser black than the surroundings. I'd never felt more relieved to see a signpost, despite it being almost impossible to read in the dark. I took a step and my foot touched solid, flat ground. A path. A change from the lumpy forest floor. It wasn't a wide path and I could see about a meter ahead. I followed the flat ground, hoping it would lead me to safety. The walking seemed endless but I felt sure I'd get out so I stuck with it, eventually stepping out into a field. I recognised a building in the distance and instantly knew where I was ... the ecology park at the edge of town, about a half hour walk from home. Fifteen minutes later I reached the road on the other side of the park ... the road home. I knew my way but it was still unnerving in the middle of the night; so silent, not one soul about. Trees swayed in the darkness and the empty fields didn't always look empty. The whole walk gave me the creeps. The last time I'd been here was when Declan had brought me in his car. Thinking of him made my nerves worse and my legs broke into a run to escape the park as fast as possible. I ran past the adventure playground where Bobby often played and on past the car park where Declan had driven me. I soon stood hands on hips, bent double, gasping for breath at the side of the road.

The walk home was horrendous. I rushed through the empty streets, the orange glow of street lights casting dim light over sleeping homes. Not one car was about and there was no sign of life. I felt I was in a ghost town. I shouldn't have woken up next to a corpse miles from home. A large ginger cat seated on a wall meowed as I passed by. I all but leapt out of my skin. Adrenaline again kicked in. I swore aloud. No one around to hear me.

After the cat episode I walked more cautiously. I was still shivering violently, my thin, short-sleeved pyjamas useless at keeping me warm. My feet ached at every step. I rubbed my arms with numb hands. I'd never before felt such bone-numbing cold. The gravel chewed up my feet. I still tasted death. Tears streamed down my frozen cheeks.

At long last ... my street. I saw my house, all the lights out, everyone asleep, no idea I was outside; that I'd been out in the woods. I tried opening the front door. Locked. I had no key with me, so how had I managed to get out? That was not my biggest worry. My shivering got worse, my teeth chattered uncontrollably. I knocked. I just wanted to be in bed. No response. I knocked harder, more urgently, my frozen knuckles stinging. Despite the pain I kept knocking, praying someone would wake up and hear me.

"Mum!" I shouted as loud as my croaky voice could muster. A light flicked on in the hall. Seconds later a figure appeared behind the patterned glass. I staggered inside into Mum's arms sobbing uncontrollably. I couldn't answer questions for a long time. I only remember saying, '*there was a body.*' She kept asking questions but I couldn't answer, not yet anyway. Gary came down. His jaw dropped at the sight of me.

"Where have you been?"

"What happened to you?"

"What body?"

"Whose body?"

"Where is it?"

The same questions over and over but I couldn't talk, couldn't think straight. I needed to not feel so cold, to stop shivering, to catch my breath, and my heart to stop pounding.

"We need to phone the police," Gary blurted out.

"We don't even know what's happened yet."

"Phone the police." I said. Mum was about to argue, then changed her mind. Gary got onto it.

"You're going to have to tell us what happened," Mum said.

"I don't know." I didn't know how I'd got to the woods or why I'd woken up there.

A short time later three hard knocks on the door announced the arrival of the police officers. Gary answered. A policeman and policewoman followed him into the living room. The policeman was tall, dark haired, in his mid-twenties. The woman was smaller with fair hair, about middle-aged. They smiled at me.

"We were told you found a body?" The woman asked. I nodded.

"We're going to ask you a few questions, okay? Answer them as best you can," The male officer said. I nodded. The door creaked open and in came Bobby, rubbing his eyes, still half asleep.

"You kept waking me up," he said to Mum. Terror washed over his little face and he turned white when he saw the police officers.

"Bobby, let's make these officers a nice cup of tea," Mum said. She took hold of his hand. He hid behind her as they walked to the kitchen. The officers sat on the sofa next to me and took out their notepads.

"Would you be able to tell me what happened?" The female officer asked.

"I woke up in the woods at the ecology park ..." I went on to tell the whole story. Seated in the warm, well lit living room my adventures of the night seemed stupid and fictional, like it hadn't happened. I couldn't get them to grasp exactly how horrific it had been. It was impossible to convey my fear. Given the absurdity of events I could have convinced myself it was only a dream, except for the taste of the corpse and my feet black with dirt and congealed blood. Mum stood behind me holding cups of tea while I spoke to the police. Bobby was drinking a beaker of warm milk, still staring in terror at the officers, not paying much attention to me.The officers looked disturbed yet remained sceptical.

"You woke up in the woods?" The female officer asked.

"Yes. I went to sleep in my bed and woke up in the woods."

"How did you get out of the house?"

"I don't know. I didn't have my key. The front door was locked."

"I'll check the back door," Gary said, and went through to the kitchen. He came back within a few seconds, a troubled look on his face.

"The back door is open, the key is still in the door, but the gate is still padlocked."

"But the gate is about six foot high," I stated.

"I know."

"So ... I managed to climb over a six foot gate in my sleep? Not possible."

"Was the back door definitely closed when you went to bed?"

"Yeah," Gary said, "I check every night. We don't leave the key in the door."

"Are you sure you weren't with anyone?" The policeman asked.

"I'm sure. There was no one else."

"And ... you weren't meeting anyone?"

"Why would I go out in pyjamas and no shoes?" I was annoyed. He thought I was lying.

"Have you ever sleep-walked before?"

"Last week," Mum said. "She was standing at the top of the stairs when I saw her. A couple of nights later she was shouting in her sleep."

"Where did you say you found the body?"

"In the woods."

"Do you know where?"

"No. It was dark. I didn't know where I was."

"How did you find the body?" And then it struck me. The realization made my blood run cold. Truth gripped me, terror swirled in my brain. I had subconsciously walked right across town and through acres of woodland in my sleep, and woken in the exact spot where the dead body lay. It was more than mere coincidence, more than sleepwalking. It was supernatural. Seemingly impossible.

"I was standing on it." I whispered, almost too frightened to say it.

"When?"

"When I woke up."

"Are you certain you saw a corpse?"

"Certain." I replied.

"How did you know what it was you were standing on?"

"I didn't. I heard a crack when I took a step. My foot sank through a pile of leaves and branches. I didn't know where I was. I'd just woken up. I used my hands to search the ground to see where I was, and that's when I saw it."

"It was dark. You were scared. Are you sure you're not mistaken? You didn't just imagine it, your mind playing tricks on you?" I knew they were doing their job, but the number of repeat questions was becoming tiresome.

"It was a dead body. I could smell it, can still taste it." They appeared to be more accepting, inclined to believe me.

"It was definitely a person and not an animal?"

"I saw its eyes and face. I didn't look for long, but definitely a person."

"I'm going to call the station to organise a search of the ecology park at dawn. Meanwhile Lorna, I suggest you go down to the hospital and get checked out."

"I'm fine."

"Just to be on the safe side. It was cold out there and you were in pyjamas. You've got quite a few scratches that need cleaning up. What do you say, Mum?"

"Definitely." Mum agreed. I said 'okay, but doubted I had any say in the matter.

"I'm sorry for waking you up little man," the policeman said to Bobby, "I'll let you go back to bed."

"I've been very good, Mr Policeman," Bobby said.

"I'm sure you have."

"So, you're not going to take me away?"

"No, we're not." He seemed happy with that.

"Are you going now?"

"Yeah. So, you be good."

"I will. Bye 'bye Mr Policeman, and lady." He trotted up the stairs to bed.

"We tell him that if he's not good the police will be after him," Mum told the officers, her face blushing.

Mum drove me to hospital. Gary stayed at home with Bobby. We sat in A&E for what felt like forever until some nurses eventually came to clean me up. My injuries stung like hell. They cleaned several bad scratches on my arms and face, where I'd fought against the branches, and bandaged my feet. There were no mirrors so I couldn't see my face, but I could feel the scratches tingling. My arms were raw, red swollen lines webbed all over the skin: they looked worse than they felt. I was surprised to see it was dawn when I walked out of the hospital. The sun was creeping out and the sky filled with spectacular shades of purple. I fell asleep in the car and woke when the engine switched off.

I put on some non-ruined pyjamas and went straight to bed. I wasn't asleep long: once Bobby woke up there was no chance of quiet. He grilled me all morning about the police and my scratches. I didn't really know what to tell him.

"Have you been naughty, Lorna?" he asked.

"No."

"Why were the police here?"

"They just wanted to ask some questions?"

"Has somebody else been naughty?"

"I don't know."

"Why do you have loads of scratches?"

"Some trees scratched me."

"How?"

"They just did."

"Were you out last night?"

"Yeah."

"Where did you go?"

"The woods ... but I was sleepwalking."

"What's sleepwalking?"

"It's when you're asleep but you walk."

"Is that why the police were here?"

"Sort of."

"Can I sleepwalk?" He carried on ... hundreds of questions. Gary eventually took him outside to play on his bike.

The police phoned later in the morning.

"What did they say?" I asked Mum after she hung up.

"They've found the body." It was what I'd expected.

"Do they know who it is?"

"Not at the moment. All they know is that it's male. They'll check dental records, age, and time of death and try and match it to anybody on the missing person's register."

"Right." I began feeling slightly nauseous, a weird tingling sensation rippling through me. When they identify the body they'll have to tell the family. He could be a son, brother, father. I'd discovered the worst possible news a family could wish to hear.

"Do they know how he died?" I couldn't stop myself asking.

"Not at the moment. A pathologist is examining the body now."

That afternoon we went out to buy a lock for my bedroom door, one that locked from the outside, so I couldn't leave my bedroom whilst asleep. Mum and Gary hadn't said much about last night. Perhaps they were as worried as me; it would explain their insistence on locking my room. It felt strangely claustrophobic - being locked in my own bedroom. I was really exhausted but couldn't sleep. I should have felt safe but I couldn't stop thinking about the previous night. I picked up my book. At long last I felt my eyelids droop, so I snuggled up under the duvet and fell into semi-consciousness.

"*Lorna.*" A male voice called my name. I jumped, startled, my eyes scanning the room for shadows or sign of the speaker.
"*You won't be able to see me.*" The voice whispered. Every muscle in my body tensed. I sat, rigid, barely breathing.
"*You found my body, in the woods, where my killer dumped me.*" This seriously freaked me out as I realised his voice was in my head. I could understand him as clearly as a thought.
"*No reason to be scared Lorna, not if you do as I ask.*" This could not be real. It was all in my head.
"*This is real Lorna, as real as your adventure in the woods last night.*" He read my every thought.
"*I am your thoughts, just as you are mine.*" How could this be happening?
"*My body was cruelly robbed from me. I need you, and you owe me. You know who killed me.*" I felt him unpicking my mind, desperate for me to identify him. I thought about Lynette's argument in the street with the woman, Mum's new shoes, the packaging they were in. I thought about the ecology park and a black jaguar. Images swirled. I began feeling sick, dizzy. A strong lemon smell knocked me back for a moment. A cleaning product ... I could taste it. Suddenly I knew. Everything fell into place. I recognised the cold, sly voice with disbelief and dread. Now I knew who the body belonged to ... Declan. I also knew his killer.
"*Well done, Lorna. I'm going to have to leave you tonight. Our adventure in the woods has drained me. Goodnight.*" I couldn't understand what was happening. Maybe I was too tired, maybe I was mad, but this couldn't be happening. Yet it all made sense. Mum had said I'd nearly thrown myself down the stairs ... *that's how he'd died*, he'd shown me the argument he and Lynette had had which had led to his death. He'd led me to his corpse. But he couldn't just take my body and steal my mind.

It wasn't right. He was dead. It was not possible. He said he'd have my life if I breathed a word, that I'd '*cost*' him his. Now he wanted revenge.

I woke from my nightmare the next day, this time in my own bed - though I could've sworn I hadn't actually slept. I went downstairs to make myself breakfast, opening all the curtains and blinds. It was bright outside. In the sunlight I questioned whether last night had really happened. I convinced myself it had been a dream, that the shock of sleepwalking into the woods and finding a body had rattled me. Then again, finding a dead body in your sleep is also practically impossible. I tried not to dwell on the matter - no time to think much about it. I was looking after Bobby while Gary took Mum to the hospital for her first ultrasound. I was excited about the baby and far too old to be afraid of nightmares.

After I'd got Bobby settled with a Power Rangers film Dad called. *What was he after*? He rarely phoned.
"Hi Lorna."
"Hi." I didn't say Dad ... Bobby was in earshot.
"How are you?" He asked.
"I'm good thanks, you?"
"I was just phoning to let you know I'm going to America in a few days ... might be gone a couple of weeks. Just thought I'd let you know in case you needed me for anything."
"Okay." If I needed anything he'd be the last person I'd consider going to. "Where are you going in America?"
"New York, business trip."
"Cool."
"You been up to much?"
"Nope, not really." Our small talk was terrible. Soon there was little else to say.
"I'll talk to you when I come back."
"Will you have a word with ..." He'd hung up before I could finish. I looked at Bobby, his eyes glued to the TV. I left the room then called Kate to see how she was.
"Are you okay?" I asked after the typical greetings.
"Yeah, I'm okay." But she didn't sound it.

"Are you still in the B&B?"

"Yeah. There's nowhere around here I can afford."

"When the baby is born Dad will have to pay, and you'll be able to find somewhere."

"It could take months though."

"He'll see sense once the baby is born. I'll make him."

"Thanks Lorna, but I don't know what you can do."

"In a few days he's off to America for a couple of weeks, but when he gets back I'll make him talk to you so you can sort things out. I promise."

"What if the baby is born while he's away?"

"Phone me and I'll get the train straight up. If you need anything tell me, and I'll come up and see you myself."

"I don't want to cause you any hassle."

"I want to look after my brother or sister. If anything happens promise me you'll call."

"I promise."

I was seriously worried about Kate. She hadn't sounded too good on the phone but I didn't know what else to do. I worried about the baby. Was she looking after herself? No matter what I said to her, I had no idea how Dad would react once the baby was born or where they'd live. I doubted a B&B would let a baby stay under its roof. My worries abated when Mum came back and showed me her scan pictures. There wasn't much to see as it was still early but I traced the basic outline of a baby. They were both so happy. I couldn't help thinking that Kate should be this happy for her child as well, but the excitement of another little brother or sister clashed with my worry. I went to work that evening, my mind a jumble of emotions.

Declan contacted me again that night, just as I was falling asleep.

"*Lorna.*" I heard my name but consciousness was slipping from me, I couldn't think straight. I tossed and turned, trying to block the voice in my head. I needed sleep, but he was preventing me. It was as though my brain had already shut down, yet still partially aware.

"*I have limited time so I won't bother with friendly greetings. You will not like what I say or what you are going to do, but neither can you prevent it.*" I kept on telling him to *"Go away!"* He never once listened. I needed sleep but his voice in my head was as clear as my own thoughts.

"You must remember the first two dreams I gave you. Think about how I was killed. I will have revenge for my death, for the loss of my spectacular future. I need my murderer to endure the suffering forced upon me. You are going to be my weapon. You are going to take revenge on my behalf. You will be my body." His voice was soft, yet vindictive. It spoke with subtle authority.

"You will help me, Lorna." And then it was gone.

Chapter 6

As soon as I woke I slipped out of bed and looked out across the street at number 4. The drive was still empty, all the curtains drawn. I hadn't seen Lynette since telling her about Declan's affair. Maybe she'd gone somewhere to hide from the world, waiting for the police. She might not know the body had been found, and that it wouldn't take long for the police to identify her husband.

Declan had told me to remember the first two dreams. I did. In the first one I'd sleepwalked to the top of the stairs where Mum had caught me before I could throw myself down. The second one was the argument during which I'd woken Bobby up with my shouting. He'd given me his recollection of his last few minutes alive. Lynette had pushed him down the stairs and he'd died. That's what he'd been trying to tell me. Lynette had buried him in the woods, and now he'd come to haunt me because I'd told Lynette about his affair. I was no longer able to convince myself I was making it up. It all made sense, right down to the parcel with Mum's shoes. Lynette hadn't opened the door to Gary, yet he'd told us about the smell of lemon disinfectant. I knew she'd killed him, but what to do with the knowledge?

I walked into the bathroom and splashed my face with cold water. In my mirror I saw brown, limp, tangled hair, and every freckle on my nose and cheeks. I looked deep into my eyes, their turquoise irises smudged with pencil grey-black webs encircling my pupils. They stared intently back at me, making sure it was still only me in there. That evening I was gradually falling asleep in front of the television.
"Lorna."
I jumped in fright. I'd not expected him to contact me while with my family. My parents were still absorbed in the programme.
"I need you to do something for me."
"Go away." I made every effort to keep any reply solely in my mind.
"You need to do something for me."
"I can't and I won't." I looked anxiously at Mum and Gary. How could they sit there, oblivious? How could they not know?
"Yes you can, and you will." I stood up and left the room. Mum and

Gary looked briefly at me and went back to watching TV. I walked up the stairs. I couldn't bare to be in the same room, with him talking to me.

"I can't bring you back from the dead, so leave me alone." I felt his anger rising.

"You are the reason I am dead!" His voice rose. I held my hands to my ears but the noise was in my head. I was going crazy.

"If you hadn't told my wife I'd still be alive. So, go back downstairs and ask your parents to take the lock off your door."

"Why?"

"I need your help."

"You only want to control me again while I sleep."

"It's the least you can do for me."

"What if I don't want to help you? What if I think you deserve to be dead?"

"You have no choice!" He bellowed. I gasped in shock, the volume! It was as though someone had roared in my ear.

"Stop playing games with me. Now, tell them not to lock your door."

"What am I supposed to say?"

"Say you don't want it locking because you need the toilet in the middle of the night. I don't care, just tell them to not lock your door."

"No."

"You cannot stop me forever."

"I can. I'll make sure someone locks the door every night before I go to sleep. I won't be able to get out."

"Play it your way then. When the time is right, the lock will not be on the door."

"You can't take it off." I was confident I'd spoiled his plan.

"I know, but you can."

"I will never do that." I was adamant.

You will one day. You'll see." Then he was gone. His words hadn't un-nerved me as they should have done. I felt certain his plan wouldn't work. For the next couple of days he contacted me nightly. Always the same message; get someone to not lock me in my room each night. Ig-noring him was impossible, yet still I refused. I soon realised he could only contact me as I was about to fall asleep, when my mind was at its weakest … well, so he'd said. He couldn't control me unless I was asleep. But I only slept in my locked room at night. Even when Mum unlocked my room around 6am (when she got up with Bobby) he couldn't control me. My mind was too strong after sleep. I felt safe but annoyed. He wouldn't leave me alone. On Thursday night I had him in my brain for hours, until he was too weak to stay. I was so tired on Friday, what with his voice keeping me awake all night. I felt I was going mad. I desperately needed a break. He was strong only because I lived metres from his murder site. If I was away from there he couldn't get to me, so I decided to go stay with Dad for a couple of days.

Lie after lie poured from my lips, uncontrollably but convincing.
"I need to go to Dad's," I told Mum when I arrived home from college.
"Why?" She looked at me, confused.
"I left my memory stick there and it has my coursework on it."
"Can't you get it another time?"
"My coursework is due in on Monday."
"Why didn't you say earlier?" She was getting annoyed.
"I didn't know. I've looked everywhere but I can't find it. I phoned Dad and he said I'd left it."
"Can't your Dad post it to you?"
"It's Friday, Mum. He'll have missed today's post and the deadline is nine o'clock Monday morning. It won't arrive by then if he posts it to . And he might forget, you know what he's like. I need it for Monday."
"Why didn't you do it earlier?"
"I did. I finished it ages ago. I was just making last minute changes when I was 'round at Dad's. I forgot all about it."
"Isn't it on your computer?"
"No. I only saved the file halfway through. No way am I doing it all again. I need to go to Dad's." I was feigning stress and anxiety.
"How will you get there?"
"Train. Dad'll pick me up at the station."
"I'm not happy about this. I wish you'd told me sooner."
"I didn't know."
"You should have printed it out."
"I know, but I forgot. I need to go to Dad's and get it."
"Fine. Okay. Do what you want." Reluctantly.
"Thanks, Mum. I'll be back Sunday. I'll be fine, promise." She had no reason to doubt me. Unknowingly she'd allowed to me go halfway

across the country, on my own, to see a pregnant ex pole-dancer and escape voices in my head. I phoned Kate straight away.

"I'm coming to see you tomorrow."

"What? Lorna, why?"

"I thought I'd see how you were as the house is free for the weekend." I wasn't going to tell her the real reason.

"You don't need to."

"I know but I want to come up."

"Honestly, you don't need to come up. I'm fine."

"I know, but I want to get away from home for a couple of days." If she asked I'd say I'd had an argument or Bobby was annoying me.

"Please, don't waste your money. I've got hospital appointments so I won't be able to see you."

"On a weekend?"

"Yeah."

"I'll come with you."

"No. You don't need to. You don't need to see me." Her tone was becoming hostile. Worrying.

"Is everything okay?"

"Yes."

"Is the baby okay?"

"Yes. Everything's fine," (I didn't believe her) "so you needn't waste time coming to see me."

"I'm not. I told you, I want to get away from my house for a couple of days."

"Come up when the baby is born, it should be soon."

"I will. But I'm coming up tomorrow as well."

"Please don't, Lorna."

"Why?" Now I was worried.

"I just don't want you wasting your time and money on me."

I wasn't buying it. "Don't worry about it. I'll see you tomorrow." I cut her off. I felt uneasy, starting to doubt her wellbeing. Maybe I was wrong to trust her, but she was carrying my brother or sister.

I spent that night researching train and bus times, eventually finding a route that would take me hundreds of miles across the country. I wrote down the times of three trains and two buses. I'd leave early in the morning, pretend to Bobby I was staying over at a friend's. Declan contacted me again that night. I'd known he would.

"The time is drawing closer, I'm nearly ready. You are to get that lock off the door." His whisper was menacing but clear. I loathed him.

"You expect me to listen and do as you say, but you don't tell me what you want me for."

"You don't want to know."

"Then, you have no chance of me taking that lock off the door."

"You will."

"I won't, so you're wasting your time. Why don't you pick on someone else? If it was so easy to tap into my brain and control my body why don't you use someone else? Find some easier target."

"It's not easy and not as simple as that. But you may get your wish and then you will find a way of removing that lock or you'll regret it."

"Is that a threat?"

"Yes, Lorna. That is a threat." Then he was gone. I promised myself I'd never remove the lock nor allow myself to be under his control again.

Chapter 7

Early next morning on the train I sent Kate a text. She replied 'not to come.' It was too late for that and besides, I didn't see her problem, it was my dad's house. On the journey I listened to music through earphones, watching the world pass by. The train rumbled through rolling green hills and fields dotted with sheep and cows. The monotonous rumbling of the train rhythmically rushing over tracks went on for hours. Passing through towns and cities I saw people going about their everyday lives amidst the noise and chaos and wondered where they were all going and why they looked so busy. Bored, I phoned Kate.

"You shouldn't be doing this. If anyone ever finds out ..."

"No one will, so there's nothing to worry about."

"You should have just rung me. I'm fine, there's no reason for you to come up."

"I wanted to make sure you're okay."

"I am." She was adamant.

"That's good then. I'll see you in half an hour."

"Lorna -"

"Bye, see you soon." I hung up. She'd be fuming but she'd get over it. Later I sent her a text. She didn't reply. Neither did she answer my calls. I caught the bus to Dad's and walked down the lane to the house. I had the passcode for the gate on my phone and the key in my bag. The house looked as amazing as ever, still as huge as I'd remembered. It felt crazy holding the key to a house this size and letting myself in. I sent Kate a text to tell her I was home, then sat down and watched a movie on the TV. She replied quickly 'on my way' despite having ignored my earlier texts and calls. Not long after, a loud roar outside grabbed my attention away from the TV. I looked out the window and saw three large motorbikes charging in through the gates. The noise of their powerful engines was disturbing in the country quiet. They pulled up on the drive. One biker had a passenger. All four people dismounted and approached the house. I stood staring, in shock. By the time I'd left the living room they were in the hallway; I'd left the door open for Kate. My heart pounded in my chest as the huge man in front of me (taller than my Dad and much taller than me) took off his helmet.

"Hello, Lorna." His voice was gruff, his black eyes looking me up and down. His face was round and scarred. A snake tattoo slithered up the side of his neck and onto his shaven head. He reminded me of a pitbull dog, solid muscle under his biking leathers.

"Who're you?" I tried disguising my terror.

"Your worst nightmare." He grinned, flashing sparkling white teeth.

"I already have one of those," I replied (Declan). His eyes glinted angrily at my cocky response. The two men alongside him removed their helmets. One was tall and black, the other smaller in height but clearly just as strong.

"It wouldn't do to get on the wrong side of me," he threatened.

"There's a right one?" My mouth curled in a slight grin. I knew I should keep quiet but wanted to look strong.

"Shut her up." He turned to the black man.

"Now!" The man took two steps and grabbed my arm tightly, his thick lips in a monstrous smile.

"No! Leave her alone." A woman? A young woman's voice. "Please, leave her alone." Behind the black man and my 'supposed' nightmare stood a smaller person. She took off her helmet.

"Kate!"

"I'm so sorry, Lorna." She stepped forward.

The wrists sticking out from her winter coat were slim, looking as though they'd snap under the slightest pressure, her fingers like twigs. She wore the same clothes she'd worn on the night I'd first seen her. Beneath the large and baggy clothes her bump was obvious. She wore no make-up. Dark rings hung under her eyes. Her skin was ghostlike and rough, clashing with her greasy hair.

"I told you not to come," she said.

"You never told me why." I was furious and completely bewildered.

"You weren't supposed to be here."

"Now that she is, we'll make her useful." The pitbull lookalike approached me.

"Where's the money?"

"I don't know."

"Where's the jewellery box?"

"My Dad doesn't own jewellery."

"He'll own a watch."

"I'm guessing he's wearing it."

"Your smart mouth is pissing me off. Either start giving me answers or I'm going to have to shut you up. Where does your Dad keep his bank details?"

"I don't know." I gritted my teeth.

"You don't seem to know an awful lot."

"This isn't my house."

"So, you won't mind if we rummage through it? T, go look through that door." The white man behind him was shorter but wider, with huge muscles on his chest and shoulders. He walked past me and into the kitchen.

"What do you want?"

"Money."

"Dad won't keep cash in the house."

"If he does, we'll find it."

"There's a locked door in here. Got a security code?" T shouted from the kitchen.

"Bring her through." The black man gripped my arm tightly and started dragging me to the kitchen.

"I can walk." He pulled even harder. My foot slipped on the polished floor and I fell awkwardly. Painful. My arm burned as he tightened his grip and continued dragging me. I tried and failed to get to my feet. When he let go of me I fell to the kitchen floor – humiliating.

"What's the code?" T asked me.

"I don't know." He slapped me, hard, across the face. My eyes shut and my cheek burned.

"Tell me the code."

"I don't know."

"Go and search the house, see if you can find anything," the Pitbull lookalike ordered.

"What's behind the door?" he asked.

"Dad's office. I've never been in there and I don't know what the code is."

"I don't believe you." T brought his face so close to mine. His breath stank.

"I'm telling the truth."

"I don't like your smart mouth. I think it lies."

"I'm not lying."

"Try the obvious. 0000, 1234, I'll get an answer off the little bitch eventually." T went back to the door and started pressing buttons.

"I don't like liars." Pitbull lookalike snarled at me.

"If I knew the bloody code I'd tell you."

"And why would you do that?"

"To get rid of you. I don't care about my Dad's money. I'd give it to you it if I knew how to."

"You're bluffing. Do I look stupid?" He shouted, spit flying from his mouth. I cowered away. He grabbed my hair and pulled hard, bending my neck backwards. Reaching into his pocket he took out a knife. I saw it for a split second then felt the blade on my neck. I struggled to get away but his grip on my hair was too tight.

"Dad never told me." I whispered. My neck hurt. Breathing was difficult.

"None of these are working," T said.

"Keep trying you imbecile."

"What's the code?" He turned back to me.

"I don't know." The pain in my neck was agonising. It felt as though my hair was being ripped from my head. Tears welled up in my eyes. I could hear faint clashing and banging upstairs. The knife was digging into my throat.

"You're a fucking useless slag," he shouted, and tugged my hair again. I fell onto my side before he let go. I screamed, curling my arms up around my neck. He slipped the knife back into his pocket.

"Break it down," he ordered. T charged the door with his shoulder. There was a great thud but the door didn't move. T cursed, rubbing his arm.

"Are you a girl or a man?" Pitbull lookalike shouted at T.

"Fuck you. You break down the bloody door." Pitbull lookalike responded by shoving his fist into the metal code box. He punched it again and again until it hung from the wall by its wires. An alarm sounded. Deafening and high-pitched. It hurt my ears.

"Bloody hell!" Pitbull lookalike shouted. Above the sound of the alarm I heard all the phones in the house ringing. He opened the door to Dad's office and stormed inside.

The furniture in Dad's office was all solid oak. He had a large black leather office chair and like the rest of the house his office was immaculate, for a brief moment anyway. Pitbull lookalike and T charged about the room, emptying drawers and cabinets, throwing out paperwork and swiping books off shelves. The alarm finally stopped but the phones went on ringing. I heard the one in the office.

"Your alarm has been tampered with. The police have been alerted." ... an automated voice from the answer machine.

"There's nothing here." T shouted, frustrated.

"Just go." The black man had run downstairs on hearing the alarm.

"The 'old bill' are coming. We're off." They ran into the hallway, ignoring me.

"Where's Kate?" The black man asked.

"Leave her. I'm not getting nicked." They ran out to their bikes. Engines fired up and they sped away.

I shut the door, locked it and headed upstairs, my heart racing. The phones still rang, pausing briefly so an automated voice on the answerphone could tell me the police were on their way. For that reason I'd left the main gate open.

"Kate." I shouted. I knew she was here, she hadn't escaped with the men.

"Kate!" I yelled louder.

"Kate!" I screamed so hard my throat turned to sandpaper. I ran up to my bedroom. I shoved open the door and the door into the en-suite and then into the adjoining bedroom searching for her. I ran back out onto the landing.

"The police are on their way and if you don't come out I'll make sure they take you away in handcuffs." I shouted again. Turning around I saw her trying to get out the front door.

"What the hell have you done?" I screamed and rushed down the stairs towards her. "The door's locked."

She blanched when she saw me. I was pleased at the terrified expression on her face.

"Please, let me out." If she wasn't pregnant I'd probably have clawed her face off. Her sad and sorry face was the last thing I could bear.

"No."

"I can't get arrested."

"So tell me ... who the fuck those men were and why were they here."

"I can't."

"You will or I'll make goddamn sure you get locked away." Her expression made me angrier. *How dare she try and look innocent?*

"You can't do that."

"Why not?"

"I'm going to have your dad's baby."

"The baby will be lucky if you get locked up. Even Dad will be a better parent than someone who's friends with men like those."

"They aren't friends." She was close to tears. I didn't care.

"Who are they?"

"Just ... people I used to know."

"Why were they here?"

"Someone I know owes them money. Your dad has money, and he owes me."

"So that makes it okay for them to hold a knife to my throat."

"You're lucky that's all they did to you."

"Lucky?" I couldn't believe it.

"Yeah, lucky your dad has a posh security system or they'd still be here." The phones were still ringing and every few seconds they'd stop to announce 'the police are on the way'. Very irritating since there were still no police. I picked up the nearest phone.

"Where are the police?" I shouted.

"We will now pass you over to a security officer at our call centre." I slammed the phone down and turned back to Kate.

"They wouldn't have been here in the first place if it wasn't for you."

"They didn't even take anything and you're not hurt. You should be thankful. They've done worse things to younger and prettier girls than you." I was close to hitting her. I wanted so badly to hit her but some shred of compassion stopped me.

"You know what they're capable of. They could have killed me without a second thought, yet you still led them here."

"You weren't supposed to be here."

"But I was and you knew it!"

"I tried telling you. I told you not to come."

"But you knew I was coming. You knew I'd be here."

"I told them, begged them not to come, not to hurt you. They didn't hurt you." I scoffed. My body was telling me different.

"You should have warned me, told me the truth."

"I couldn't." Now she was crying. Tears rolled down her cheeks. "They wouldn't let me. They would have hurt me and the baby. I wanted to but I couldn't. You don't know them, you don't know what they're capable of."

"But you do. And you still invited them here."

I head sirens. *Finally!* Kate also heard. Her face went from white to an almost green colour.

"Please Lorna, don't tell them I was involved." She was talking fast. "It's my ex, Jamie. He had a drug problem, ran into debts with the dealers ... the three that were here. He did some dodgy work for them to pay it off but got busted and lost thirty grand's worth of stuff. They want his blood. They've already stabbed him and they want their money. Jamie had no one else. I have no money but your Dad does. I just thought if they got their money from here they wouldn't kill him. Your Dad can claim on his insurance or whatever. He owes me anyway, and you weren't supposed to be here. No one was meant to get hurt." She rushed her words. The police car pulled up outside. Two officers walked to the door. I took the key out of my pocket and pushed past Kate to unlock the door. I told the police everything. I wasn't lying for her sake. They arrested her. All she did was cry.

"It wasn't my fault. I didn't have a choice. I don't know who they are." She sobbed but didn't struggle as they led her to the car. One officer stayed with me while they waited for the forensic team. He phoned my Dad to inform him of the break-in ... I didn't dare. I gave the officer the same excuse I'd given my mum about the memory stick, which he relayed to my Dad when he questioned my being there. At least nothing had been taken. Dad would have killed me.

Forensics arrived and took a photo of my neck. The knife had left barely a scratch but it was sufficient proof a knife had been held to my throat. My arm was bruised from the grip of one of the men; they took a photo of that as well. They took photos of Dad's trashed office. I didn't think anything had been taken. They were there for ages looking for fibres and fingerprints. The officer got a phone call from the station. They'd released Kate. I was furious, especially when they said she hadn't given any names or details. The officer told me she'd said they'd threatened her because her ex owed money, that she'd had no choice or they'd have hurt her and the baby. Apparently they hadn't given her their names and she didn't know where they lived. She also said she'd tried telling them not to come when you were there but they hadn't listened.

"She's lying. Of course she knows who they are."

"Did she attack you?"

"No."

"Did she take part in the robbery?"

"No."

"She said she tried to stop them from hurting you."

"Yeah, but that's not the point! She led them here, knowing I was here, and didn't tell me. She knows they could have hurt me."

"We will investigate, but until we have something else to go on we can't charge her." I was so angry but he wasn't about to re-arrest her. I was allowed to clean up after forensics were done. I told the police I'd be okay by myself. I wasn't. I was a nervous wreck, but needed to be alone. I was glad when everyone had left. I tidied upstairs and cleaned up broken glass from a lampshade. I put Dad's socks back in a chest of drawers they'd knocked over, and made up the beds where the duvets had been thrown aside. I picked up all of Dad's paperwork in his office and stacked it in neat piles on his desk. I placed books back on shelves. Within an hour you wouldn't have known there'd been an armed robbery.

Dad phoned twice. I left my phone to ring. I had a text from Kate saying 'Sorry. X.' I wanted to send a nasty reply but thought better of it. Dad rang again. This time I couldn't ignore him.

"Lorna."

"Dad."

"Are you okay?" I couldn't lie and say I wasn't surprised that he asked after me first.

"Yeah."

"What are you doing at the house?" I repeated my story about the memory stick. I think he believed it.

"Did they hurt you?"

"Not really."

"Lorna, tell me exactly what happened."

"I came into the house. After a few minutes I heard bikes. I'd only just got in so the gate was still open. They rode straight up to the house. Three bikes and a woman, the pregnant one who'd come round the first night I stopped over. She was with them as a passenger on one of the bikes. She said you were rich, that you owed her." Then I told him the rest, but part lying. I didn't tell him I knew Kate or that I'd opened the gate for her, but the rest was true. He'd find out eventually, when he got back to England and contacted the police, but I didn't dare tell him then, not over the phone.

"I'm needed in America for over a week. Before you leave make sure the gate and doors are locked and the alarms turned back on."

"I will. Everything is locked now."

"Does your Mum know yet?"

"No."

"She's going to kill me."

"It's not your fault." Mum would definitely blame him. That's why I wasn't going to tell her. He didn't need to know that.

"Lorna, I have to go back into the office now. Stay safe and I'll phone you later, I promise."

"Okay, 'bye Dad."

I was so relieved he wasn't angry, I'd even wanted him to stay on the phone. After he'd hung up I looked around the empty house. I felt so alone and scared. I checked countless times that the gate was shut and doors and windows locked. I couldn't settle down sitting and watching TV, but I didn't want to leave the safety of the house. It wasn't long and my phone rang again. Kate. I let it ring briefly before deciding to answer.

"Lorna?" I was relieved to hear her voice instead of those men.

"Yes." I replied.

"The police phoned social services. They've just been round to see me."

I could have told her I didn't care, but that would have been a lie. I cared about what happened to my future brother or sister.

"What did they say?"

"I think they're going to take the baby off me." Her voice broke. I heard a sob. I felt like saying 'good.' I didn't want my brother or sister to have a mother like her, involved with people like them. But neither did I want my brother or sister growing up in care, in a strange family, not knowing me or Bobby.

"Lorna, you've got to drop the charges against me. You've got to tell them I didn't do anything."

"You haven't even been charged."

"But I will be. If I don't talk they will charge me, and then they'll take my baby off me."

"So talk. Tell the police who the men are."

"I can't!" She exclaimed.

"Why not?"

"They'll kill me, they'll kill Jamie."

"They can't kill anyone behind bars."

"There's more than just them three. They know people, dangerouspeople who'll break your leg for a laugh, and the won't be behind bars forever."

"So why the hell did you meet them? Why did you bring them here, to me?"

"To help Jamie."

"Why do you care about your ex from ages ago? Why do you care about some idiot pusher who messes with the wrong people? I'm not helping you. I'm not helping someone who puts the life of some guy before their child."

"You've got to help me. I'm carrying your brother or sister."

"How do I know you're not lying? How do I know you're not just pretending it's Dad's kid to get his money? You could just be saying that so I get you out of trouble."

"You sound like your fucking father!" The words hit me as hard as any punch. A wave of fury washed over me.

"I am *nothing* like him." I gritted my teeth. "I helped you. I helped you when I didn't have to. I cared about you and you nearly got me killed for it."

"You helped me when it suited you, and now you don't give a damn." I wanted to scream, call her a stupid, ungrateful cow.

"Yeah, you're right. I don't give a damn about you. But I do care about the baby, whether it's my brother or sister or not. So, are you safe? Are

62

they going to come back and hurt you?"

"They don't know where I'm staying. I told them to meet me at the train station at the next town away from here."

"Am I safe here? Are they going to come back?"

"I doubt it. They won't want to risk it, and they live too far from here to bother again. They've got nothing against you or your dad, besides, the house is too secure." That should have made me feel safer. It didn't.

"What happens if Jamie needs your help again?" There was a long pause ...

"He's past my help now. If they see me again they'll kill me, think I led them into a trap ... bringing them to your house. I can't help him anymore."

"What will happen to him?" No answer.

"You're not going to help me, are you?"

"I'm not going to lie to the police. I can't drop any charges. They burgled Dad's house and he knows it was because of you. You put my life at risk and he isn't going to let you get away with it."

"I'm glad you didn't get hurt." That hurt.

"I know."

"Bye, Lorna."

"Bye."

Fear remained. All night I felt like a child, scared of the dark, of being alone. I could no longer trust Kate, nor her word that they wouldn't come back for me. I spent the night alone in my bed in the empty house. I was devastated by Kate's betrayal. Anger returned whenever I considered what could have happened to me. I listened out for the growl of bikes. Fortunately I heard no voices in my head for which I was grateful. My thoughts were mine alone.

I left early the next day, triple checking that all the doors and windows were locked before leaving. I made sure the gate was firmly shut before walking down the lane. Waiting at the bus stop alone, on a long stretch of road, I felt exposed. One bike raced down the road and my heart jumped. It continued on past me. Relief. I felt much safer once on the bus and then finally on the train home.

I was looking forward to getting home. I opened the front door and walked into the living room. Gary was lying on the sofa, looking down at the floor … crying. I had never seen him cry. I paused a few awkward seconds not knowing what to do. It felt like I was intruding. About to step back out of the living room he looked up and saw me.

"Lorna." He looked surprised and sat up, hurriedly wiping his eyes.

"Where's Mum ... and Bobby?"

"Bobby's at my Mum's." Only half an answer.

"What's happened?" Grown men do not cry over nothing.

"Sit down, Lorna." I sat, suspicious.

"Your mum is in hospital." I felt a heavy weight drop into my stomach. He continued before I could respond. "She's okay. I promise, she's okay."

"What happened?" I was angry he hadn't told me sooner and that no one had phoned me. I knew I was giving him an accusing look but he looked guilty. I was already blaming him for something I knew nothing about.

"She miscarried." His voice rose in pitch, sounding as though he couldn't breathe. I stood rooted to the spot, all anger fled.

"I'm sorry." I didn't know what else to say. Numbness seeped through me.

"It's not your fault. It's no one's fault. Sometimes these things just happen."

"You should be with Mum."

"They wouldn't let me." He sounded bitter.

"We can visit her tomorrow."

"I should be with her now." His voice was hoarse.

"Can she come home tomorrow?"

"Yeah."

"That's good. At least Mum is okay." But I knew she'd be feeling far from okay. "What have you told Bobby?"

"He knows the baby has gone. He didn't really understand ... asked a lot of questions I didn't know how to answer."

"He's not going to understand." I certainly couldn't.

I made him a cup of tea then took a bath. The numb feeling remained. I lay in the water, warm, just me and my thoughts. I knew I shouldn't, but I couldn't help thinking that Mum and Gary deserved a baby more than Kate and Dad. It felt like choosing between siblings, but I didn't trust Kate and the world she'd got herself involved with. I also knew how terrible a parent Dad was. I lay in the bath until the water turned cold then went to bed. I'd anticipated a voice but none came, not even as I drifted off. I should have felt relieved, but couldn't help thinking something was wrong. Declan was always in my head when I slept here, mere metres from where he'd been killed. At Dad's house I was too far away. Why wasn't he with me tonight? He wouldn't have forgotten. Yet another night passed in silence.

When I went downstairs for breakfast Gary was still laying on the sofa, last night's empty mug of tea still in his hand, resting on his stomach. Mouth open, his chest rose and fell. He woke, startled, when I walked past.

"Morning," I greeted.

"Morning." He grunted. I took his mug and made us toast. The hospital phoned early, me still in my pyjamas, to let Gary know he could fetch Mum. I dressed quickly. Soon we walked into the hospital, up to Mum's ward. She was sitting up on the bed, glaring at Gary as he walked in.

"I can't believe you ... last night," she said, a sharp edge to her words.

"It was that snobby receptionist. She wouldn't let me stay with you."

"So you decided to shout the place down and show us up?"

"She was a cow." *'Visiting hours end at 6:30p.m. I will not permit visitors to see patients after that time on my ward. You'll have to leave.'* He imitated the woman behind the desk, in a high pitched pompous voice. "Who the devil does she think she is? *Her ward.* She's only a bloody receptionist. I only told her where to stick her visiting hours and she threatened to call security."

"The whole ward – in fact the whole bloody hospital – heard where she should stick her visiting hours."

"I needed to be with you."

"Did you think I needed a performance like that?" I'd *'enjoyed'* the look Mum was giving him many a time ... it was the last thing he needed right then.

"We got you some chocolates," I said. We'd stopped off at a petrol station on the way. I'd picked the biggest box. She looked at me for the first time since we'd arrived.

"Thanks." She smiled but it wasn't soft enough to tell that her anger

65

had gone. The last thing I wanted was for her and Gary to fight.

"I'm sorry, Mum."

"It's not your fault." From the look she was still giving Gary I was about to say it wasn't his fault either, but stopped short.

"Did you get your memory stick from your Dad's?" Mum asked. I had to think for a second ... I'd forgotten what she was on about.

"Yeah, I did." I lied.

"So why aren't you in college? I thought your deadline was today."

"It is, but I can email it to my teacher."

"You should be in college."

"I wanted to see how you were."

"I'm fine." She couldn't have been fine; not possible after what had happened to her. I said nothing. Mum made to stand up. Gary stepped forward to help but she backed away for a second, rejecting his help but I saw her flinch in pain. She let Gary take her arm. "I just need to get out of this hospital." A nurse came to discharge her, giving her a pile of leaflets. We passed the receptionist on the way out of the ward.

"You're lucky we let you back in after yesterday," she said to Gary in a manner far too posh for her accent, her pinned up hair pulling back the wrinkles from her face. Mum dragged Gary silently past.

"She is a cow," I whispered to Gary.

"Did you see her smug little toad face? Too far up her own backside that one." He muttered insults all the way out of the hospital.

Mum made me go to college. I had to go home and pretend to get my history folder and coursework, even though I didn't have a history lesson that day;. I'd submitted the coursework the month before. I sat in Geography class wondering what the hell I was doing there and chatting to my friend Hannah. It felt surreal. I couldn't believe the world had gone on as normal over the weekend while Mum had been in hospital and I'd had a knife held to my throat in an armed robbery. My teacher was waffling on about peri-glacial landscapes. It was even more difficult than normal to concentrate. How had I ever thought that learning the names of different piles of rocks meant anything to me? I spent the day feeling I didn't belong. College was too normal. My life was full of secrets and fear which didn't belong within the whitewashed walls of this building or ordinary lives of my friends.

66

My night times however, were beginning to feel normal. Falling asleep that night my thoughts were completely my own. I hadn't sleepwalked since finding his body and he hadn't contacted me since I'd been at Dad's. Maybe he'd actually gone and I could sleep in peace.

I was descending into the depths of a since-forgotten dream when I shot bolt upright, arms outstretched, eyes wide open, panic surging through my veins - but nothing associated with my dream. There was no reasonable explanation for the sudden awakening. The darkness of my room closed in on me, not a shadow distinguishable in the solid mass of black. The curtains, for once, succeeding in blocking out the orange glare from the streetlights outside. I heard movement ... the small click of a lock. My bedroom door creaked open. I stared anxiously as dim light from the landing washed into my room. My heart hammered in my ears. A shadow fell across the floor ... a figure approached me. My eyes travelled from the shadow to the figure ... shock and relief. Even in the dark I easily recognised Bobby.

"Bobby! You frightened the life out of me. What's wrong?" I could feel myself relaxing.

"You haven't yet done what I have asked. You will pay the price of your disobedience." I stared, horrified, at the small face of my three year old brother, speaking in the voice of a man. A dead man. *"You have failed in your task. Now you must suffer the consequences. I gave you a warning, Lorna. I gave you my word. And my word is the truth, my promise."* This was worse than any nightmare. *"You will do as I say or the cost will be great ... your brother's life."* As my eyes grew accustomed to the dim light I saw the rigid body of my little brother, his deadpan expression unlike any I had ever seen. Dark, dead eyes staring unseeing at me. His figure black, framed by the yellow light from the landing, his shadow crept from the floor up onto my bed.

"You wouldn't ... ?" my voice barely a whisper. He laughed, a deep sound, heavy with danger. The boy in front of me threw his head back in synchronised laughing, evil radiating from his face.

"I wouldn't? Don't be so sure. How do you think your mother's baby died? It was easy, of course, the baby - if you could call it one – wasn't even properly formed. Not at all difficult to kill given the power of my fully grown spirit. I need you to do what I ask." Those words could not be coming from my

Bobby, but his lips were moving. The voice, this time, came audibly from his mouth, not in my head.

"No … you … you will always be dead. No matter how many people you kill you will always be dead, so what's the point?" He couldn't do that to my family, much less to my brother.

"The point is revenge. I need revenge. I will not go on without revenge." Bobby's face distorted into a smirk. I felt sick. I wanted to scream, cry, and shake him until the evil left, save my little brother, but I was too frightened to touch him.

"Your brother will suffer the same fate as your unborn sibling if you do not remove the lock. I could easily make him strangle himself." Bobby's hand reached for his throat. *"Or I could make him jump in front of a lorry."* Bobby jumped one step towards me. I shuffled back in my bed, terrified.

"Do it now. The door is unlocked, so do whatever you need me for now, just don't hurt my brother." I pleaded. I didn't even ask what he wanted me for. I didn't want to know.

"Not tonight. I don't have much strength left for tonight. Breaking minds is hard work. But soon. And I promise you, Lorna, this door must not be locked again or your brother will suffer the consequences."

A mind-bending scream erupted from Bobby's mouth. His hands gripped his head and he sank to the floor. I jumped up off my bed to pick him up. His tiny body squirmed and thrashed about on the floor. I managed to lift him and he went limp in my arms. I heard noises from Mum's bedroom and within seconds Gary was with me.

"Lorna. What's going on?"

"I … I …" I couldn't string two syllables together. Gary flicked on the light. I laid Bobby on my bed, limp arms and legs sprawled all over. I was thankful he looked at least normal, instead of the rigid, robot-like little boy I'd heard minutes earlier. I was relieved, when he opened his eyes, to see they were blue and darting around the room, except now they showed terror instead of loathing.

"Bobby, what's wrong son?" He briefly glanced at Gary before answering, "The man said that if Lorna doesn't do as she's told he will hurt me." His words trembled. He was shivering.

"What man, Bobby?"

"The man that Lorna knows." Gary's looked to me for an explanation.

I attempted my best confused look and shrugged my shoulders.

"You were dreaming, Bobby, that's all." I smiled and ruffled his hair. Gary then relaxed. Bobby looked at us horror-stricken.

"No! It wasn't a dream. He said he would hurt me. He really did."

"I don't know any man. It was just a dream, you were asleep." Bobby gave me a pleading look, desperate for understanding.

"No one's going to hurt you Bobby. You're safe here with me and your Mum. There's nothing to worry about and Lorna will do as she's told, won't you Lorna?"

"Yeah, I will. I promise I'll do as I'm told." I looked Bobby in the eyes, hoping he'd realise I had actually understood him.

When I woke in the morning I knew it was time ... time to break my promise to never take the lock off my door. Looking at Bobby's innocent face over breakfast I knew I had to do it.

"Morning." I greeted Mum, seated on the sofa with a mug of coffee.

"Morning. What was wrong with Bobby last night?" She whispered his name so he wouldn't hear from the dining table.

"He just had a bad dream."

"That's what Gary said. He said it had really 'creeped' him out."

"Yeah, but he looks okay now." Bobby was slurping the milk from his bowl and it ran down his chin onto his pyjamas.

"Bobby! Do you have to do that?" Mum exclaimed. He put his bowl back on the table and wiped his mouth with his sleeve.

"Those pyjamas were new on last night young man." Mum stood up and went to get a wipe. She seemed okay this morning, looking much less tired than the day before. I went into the kitchen and found one ... a screwdriver, in a pot under the sink.

"What do you want that for?" Mum asked.

"I'm going to take the lock off my door."

"Oh, okay." I tried to conceal my alarm. *Was that it? ... 'Oh, okay'. No awkward questions, no warnings?*

"It's just that I can't get out of my room on a night when I need the loo. The night you were in hospital I was fine. Gary had forgotten to lock it. I don't think I've sleep-walked since the night I got outside." The night I found *his* body. I felt a need to explain my reasons for taking the lock off.

"Okay." That was all she said. I stared at her in disbelief. Had she forgotten about the body? How could she have forgotten ... the reason for the lock was to protect me, so I couldn't do anything dangerous? My finding the body had not been mentioned since - but so easily forgotten? I certainly hadn't. But, of course, she didn't understand exactly what she was letting me do. I watched Bobby squirming away as she tried to wipe his mouth and knew I had to get that lock off. Deep down I guess I wanted her to stop me, because one night Declan could do anything to me.

Every night I lay awake, terrified. I couldn't believe I'd done it. The door was unlocked. Declan could get me in my sleep any night. Surprisingly, for the next week I woke to my alarm every morning and nothing had happened. What was he waiting for? He could have used me the night Mum had been in hospital, with the door unlocked. I speculated he daren't have me leave the house while Gary slept on the sofa downstairs in case he heard. The wait was making me sick, especially him leaving me alone all week. The police phoned on Friday.

"Is this Lorna?" A male voice. He sounded old.

"Yes."

"This is the police. We have identified the body." My stomach knotted.

"Okay." I tried keeping an even tone.

"The body is that of a Mr Declan Rhodes, one of your neighbours. He lived at number 4 on your street. You know him?" The officer's voice had taken on an accusatory tone.

"Not really."

"We may need to question you again."

"I've told you everything I know." My heart was hammering, blood pounded in my ears.

"We're now investigating a murder. You may be able to clarify some things for us."

"Okay." I didn't know what else to say.

"We have taken in Mr Rhodes' wife for questioning today. She's been released pending further investigation." Of course that was bound to happen, but I needed to know if she'd mentioned my name, to know what she'd said.

"I cannot stress enough ... you may not contact Mrs Rhodes during the investigation nor disclose the identity of the body until we have released the information publicly."

"Can I tell my parents?"

"You may. We'll be in touch soon. Bye, Lorna."

"Bye."

Mum had been watching and hounded me the minute I replaced the phone on the cradle.

"What did they say?"

"They've identified the body."

"Who was it?"

"Lynette's husband. Declan."

"No!" She looked horrified. She told Gary when he got in from work.

"You're not allowed to tell anyone else," I told them.

"Do they know the killer?" Mum asked.

"No. They questioned Lynette today but she's been released."

"There's no way Lynette would have done it," Mum said.

"Maybe it was the mistress?" Gary said.

"How did he die?"

"Don't know."

"I can't believe he's dead."

The debate over 'whodunit' would keep them gossiping for hours but I didn't want to talk about it. I didn't trust myself not to let slip what I knew. I didn't want to think about his death or his body, and least of all Lynette. It was going to happen that night … I just knew it.

Chapter 8

Panic rose. I tried regaining control. Fierce dread flooded my every cell. My struggle for control slipped. My plan had failed and there was nothing I could do. Panic abruptly disappeared. Calm returned. The pressure in my head disappeared, my senses functioned again. I felt good, but awfully confused. When I opened my eyes I realised I was standing upright. Precious seconds ticked by as I gawked at my surroundings yet knew exactly where I was ... number 4 ... at the bottom of the stairs where Declan had died. I'd suspected he'd bring me here, where he'd be strongest. Wrong. I was back in control. A flicker of light sizzled across the floor towards me, a spark following an invisible string. In a matter of moments it would reach the petrol I'd poured on the floor, not that I could remember doing it.

The petrol canister! Still in my hand! I threw it down the hallway like a grenade, aiming for the kitchen door. It landed with a clatter at the back of the kitchen. Then, I noticed in fright that my hands were covered in petrol! If I moved any part of that string I would burn along with the house. There was nothing else for it; I had to move. I spun around the banister, placed my left foot on the bottom step and hoped against all hope I'd make it up to the top before the spark met the petrol. I charged up three steps at a time, not daring to pause or look back, and dashed for the back bedroom.With only one foot on the upper landing it blew. The explosion deafened me. The blast slung me forward into a wall. Explosion after explosion tore through the house. I lay flat on the floor, crawling forward on my elbows, head down. The fire hissed furiously, raging through the house, spitting sparks and burning debris onto my back, my cries inaudible. I soldiered onward, not looking back, knowing that flames were edging towards my feet. Pushing all thought from my mind, I focused solely on the bedroom door. The smoke was stifling. I struggled for breath, on the brink of collapse, but nearing the door. I carried on crawling, ignoring the sounds of the house collapsing. I reached for the door-handle and wrapped my fingers around it. I yelped in pain. It was scorching hot. Using fingertips on my left hand I gripped the metal and twisted, biting my bottom lip through the pain. The door opened into the master bedroom, as I'd known it would. This house had the same layout as ours and this was the room where Mum and Gary slept. I crawled in, kicking the door shut to hold back the flames and smoke a little longer. Staying low I edged over to the bed where Lynette sat, bundled up in a duvet, shaking.

"Get up!" I shouted. My throat felt like it had been torn to shreds. She looked at me droopy-eyed, expressionless. I spotted them. Sleeping tablets. She'd drugged herself. Whether to sleep or escape guilt or fear I didn't know. It quickly dawned on me I was risking my life for a murderer. I dragged myself up onto my knees beside her and shook her arm. She looked at me, but didn't move. The room was fast filling with smoke ... no time to be nice. Using all my strength I slapped her hard on one cheek. She gasped, eyes widening.

"We need to get out." She just stared, dumbfounded, still half asleep. I flung back the duvet. She was still fully dressed in joggers and a T-shirt. Grabbing her wrist I pulled her from the bed. She didn't resist, managing to stand briefly before falling to her knees. She was completely out of it. I was fast losing patience.

"Your house is on fire! We must get out." I could hear flames licking at the door. I'd thrown the petrol can into the kitchen immediately below. I could feel the smothering heat and knew the fire was raging downstairs, eating away at the ceiling - my floor, and prayed it would hold until we were out. I saw Lynette breaking out of her daze. She stared, horror etched in her every feature. But she was weak, shaking, and still didn't attempt to move.

"Lynette, we've got to get out." I wrapped her left arm over my shoulders to help her over to the window. My eyes streamed, stinging horrendously, unable to resist the smoke. I gasped for rapidly depleting oxygen. Smoke hit the back of my throat and I retched. Lynette was wriggling to free herself of my grip.

"No. No. No!" She shouted. I looked at her pointing towards her bedroom door. I shook my head.

"My sister. Ben." She looked at me desperately. I just dragged her to the window. She hadn't the energy to fight and I didn't know what she was talking about. Exhausted, we made it to the window. I stood up, supporting myself on the windowsill, then pushed hard on the window glass until it had fully opened. I gulped down the air in between coughing and spluttering, like surfacing in a swimming pool. I turned back to Lynette, lying on the floor. Smoke now filled the room … I couldn't even see the bed. I saw she'd sat up under the window. She looked up at me.

"Ben … Ben … get Ben …" *What was she trying to tell me*? She whispered more urgently. "Please … Ben … Ben." She began coughing violently. I felt she didn't have long left. I started lifting her up and she pulled herself up against the window.

"Take some deep breaths. You've got to climb onto the windowsill."

"Ben …" She looked at me desperately. I knew she wouldn't leave without an answer.

"Who's Ben?" I asked, my voice ragged.

"… nephew," she breathed, "him and my sister are here." Black smoke billowed out through our window.

"They're in the house?" She nodded. I looked for the door. All I could see was thick black smoke. The heat was overwhelming. It felt as though my skin was melting. Each breath burnt my throat and lungs.

"They've got out," I answered. She smiled weakly. She really believed me. I hoped she was confused from the drugs, hallucinating about Ben and her sister. I couldn't help them anyway, even if they were here. I helped her up onto the windowsill, though she seemed more able now that she considered her family safe. She swung her body around, dangling her legs outside. I heard shouts outside. I looked. People were pointing up at her, neighbours gathering around to see the fire. I heard screams in the distance.

"She's around the back!" Paul, a neighbour, yelled out to the others on the street. The crowd in the number 4 back garden grew. I recognised almost all the faces. Flames were leaping out of the window to the right of the back door, but none below our window - not yet anyway.

"Lynette!" Paul shouted. "Turn around so you're facing the house. Dangle as far down as you can. I'll catch you." She nodded.

"Hold onto the window frame and turn around, I'll support you,." I told her. She inched around on the sill. I held her steady. Her knees rested on the frame outside and her hands inside. I clutched her shoulders tightly. Because of the smoke and her body blocking the view no one else could see me.

"Take one knee off the frame and dangle your leg down. I'll catch you if you fall," Paul shouted. She was shaking violently. I nodded to her. Tears poured from her eyes; she was terrified.

"I'm going to hold you steady, I won't let you go until you're ready," I assured her. She moved one knee off the windowsill and wobbled slightly as she dropped down. A frightened moan escaped her lips.

"It's okay, I won't let you fall."

"There's someone else up there!" I heard a woman shout.

"I see them. There is someone else there." Someone replied.

"Lynette, you've got to lower the other leg now." Paul shouted up but he was looking at me. Lynette trembled so much at one point I thought she would fall, but she quickly put the knee back onto the windowsill. "Just put your knee down and drop. I can't hold you much longer." She whimpered and whined. Sirens? At last. I couldn't wait for the emergency services. My arms were wrapped under her armpits and my hands clasped together around her back but I couldn't hold on forever. She lowered her back and removed her knee from the frame. She fell, fast, almost pulling me out with her. She let out an ear-splitting scream but I managed to keep her from falling all the way down. She still clung to the windowframe - barely.

"Lorna!" Gary. Lynette's fingers slipped from the frame. She shrieked. I let go. Paul wasn't ready, too busy looking at me. She fell on top of him. They lay in a heap on the ground. People screamed and rushed forward. Gary yelled.

"Lorna!" Paul stood up and helped Lynette to her feet. I screamed. Fire ripped into the room. I jumped up onto the windowsill as the floor collapsed. Fire spewed out of the French doors downstairs.

"Lorna!" Gary roared. Everyone fled to the back of the garden. Paul picked up Lynette. Gary knocked a neighbour aside and stood on the grass, as close as he dared. Flames scorched my back, crept up my neck, burnt my hair. I leapt …

The ground rushed to meet me. Stomach churning. Gary's outstretched arms waited for me. He staggered back but didn't fall. Quickly regaining his balance he ran me to the crowd at the back of the garden just as the windows blew outwards. Fire billowed out into the night, engulfing the house. He turned and wrapped his arms around me, hugging me tight, my face against his chest, shielding me from the fire. "What the bloody hell did you think you were doing?" He asked, exasperated, possibly annoyed, but highly relieved. I couldn't answer. The wailing of sirens grew louder. A shrill screech filled the air ... Lynette had managed to break free of Paul's grasp, racing towards her house. A neighbour grabbed her before she got too near.

"Ben! Claire!" She cried, screaming out their names, over and over. "They're in there. Ben!" Paul and Stu, along with other neighbours, struggled to hold her back. I broke away from Gary and staggered over to Lynette. Her uncontrolled howling tore at my heart. Gary called my name: I ignored him. Lynette stared at me intently, seemingly unable to speak, but her wailing paused briefly.

"I didn't know they were in there." Sirens blared in the night. Lynette crumpled to the ground, no energy left to scream. I bent down to her. "What bedroom were they in?"

"The front one." They hadn't stood a chance. I said nothing. The petrol had been placed right beneath the front bedroom. If the explosion hadn't ripped apart the floor, the fire would have torn through the room in seconds.

"Claire, my sister, didn't want me to be alone tonight, not after what had happened with the police." I'd thought it was the drugs. No one else had lived in the house, not since killing her husband. I really had not believed, or even considered, that someone else was in the house. Looking at the wreck of a woman in front of me, I knew. I'd been wrong.

"He's five years old." She sobbed, trembling from head to foot. I stared in horror at the blazing fire, all hope lost.

Firemen charged around the side of the house, paramedics in tow. They made straight for Lynette, quickly wrapping a blanket around her and sitting her up on the grass. They gave her an oxygen mask. A fireman spotted me, my eyes glued on the flames licking away at the house.

"Were you in there?" I nodded. He called for a paramedic. Gary walked towards me.

"There's still two people in there," I told him. He looked at the fire then sharply back at me.

"You sure? We were told there was only one person in the building."

"The woman's sister and nephew were sleeping over. Her nephew's only five ... she's just told me." He looked at the fire in disbelief.

"There's still two people in there. One, a five year old boy." He called over to the other firemen. One shook his head. The remaining team turned towards the fire. My neighbours gasped in unison, looking back and forth at one another and the fire, their faces ashen.

"No chance," said of them, bluntly.

"No one can still be alive. Half the house has collapsed," said another.

"We can't risk it. Impossible."

"Just get the hoses and control it before it spreads to next door." The decision pained him. I could tell it was not in his nature to do nothing, to not even try, but it was obvious ... no one could still have been alive in there.

He turned back to me. "We need to get you to hospital."

"I'm fine."

"How long were you in the fire for?"

"I don't know. It seemed ages, but probably only a couple of minutes."

"Best get you to hospital, just to check you over. It won't do you any harm." I nodded. A paramedic came forward. They'd already taken Lynette away. The fire team had set to work preparing their hoses. Police (I hadn't noticed them before) ushered the crowd out onto the street away from the fire crew.

"Can I take Lorna to her mum first, before we go?" Gary asked.

"Yeah, that's fine." Gary and the paramedic helped me from the garden out to the street and guided me to our house. Gary opened the front door. I stepped into the front room, the paramedic following.

"Lorna!" Mum rushed towards me and pulled me into a lung-crushing hug. "I was so worried! When we woke to the fire and you weren't in your room I thought you might have been sleep-walking again. Where were you?" I didn't answer at first. That's when she stepped back to search my face for answers. She turned to Gary, her eyes piercing him. His face had a blackened look about it but it wasn't conspicuous, and his joggers and t-shirt didn't look that damaged either. I looked down at myself. My arms and hands were black, as were my previously purple pyjamas. The visible skin on my bare feet (that I could see) was red and the backs of my ankles blistered.

"Please tell me ... Lorna, do not tell me you were in there." She looked through our front room window at the blazing fire.

"Gary, was she in there?" Her voice, barely audible, had the harshest edge to it.

"The important thing is, she's okay," Gary replied. I could tell he was terrified. Mum was going to hit the roof.

"We really must get going to the hospital," the paramedic said.

"Mum, I'm fine, I promise. I'm just going to get checked over, Gary can come with me. You stay here with Bobby and go back to sleep." Before she could say another word I gave her a quick kiss on the cheek and we left the house, sharpish.

The fire sizzled and hissed as jets of water soused it. Nothing was working; the fire still blazed high into the sky. I took a last look as I climbed into the ambulance. I had started it. I had killed two people. It hadn't sunk in yet. I sat down on the bed, Gary next to me, the paramedic on the seat in the corner.

"Mum is going to kill me," I said to Gary.

"It's only because she loves you."

"I know ..."

"Why did you go into the fire?"

"I don't know, wasn't really thinking," I mumbled. This was the conversation I'd dreaded ever since reaching the safety of the back garden. I knew there'd be question after question but I hadn't thought up a convincing lie.

"Lorna, I don't understand. How did you get in there so fast? The explosions woke up the whole street. At that point half the house had blown up and there was no way anyone could have climbed the stairs. Your mum and I went into your bedroom to see what was happening. You weren't there so I went to see if you'd run to the fire. The front door was open, your key still in it. I was one of the first there and couldn't see you. There was no way into the house." Gary looked accusingly at me. I knew I'd have to explain myself. So, I made up the story as I went along.

"I couldn't sleep. Standing at my window, looking over the street, I saw something at number 4, didn't know what at first. Then I realised it was fire. I wasn't really thinking straight so I grabbed my key, rushed downstairs, opened the front door and ran to the house. The back gate was open, so was the back door. I went inside and the fire was in the front room. There was smoke around the stairs but the flames hadn't reached the staircase. I only ran up the stairs because I thought it was still safe. When I reached the top of the stairs the whole house exploded. I managed to make it to the back bedroom where Lynette was. I didn't know anyone else was in the house." I knew the story was flimsy and if it was discovered the fire had begun in the hallway, and started by string being set alight my story would fall apart. I hoped all the evidence would have burnt up and prayed no one would ever suspect me of arson. Gary looked into my eyes, unsure whether or not to believe me. I think he decided I was telling the truth. I had no reason to lie, or so he thought.

"Are you in any pain?" the paramedic asked.

"Not really." I was in a lot of pain but I didn't want any drugs. My body felt battered and weak, different pains attacking every part of me.

"How's your breathing?"

"Fine, I think." It wasn't perfect but I could talk, so I guessed I was okay.

"I can get you a mask."

"I'm okay."

Gary spoke after a quiet spell. "You did a heroic thing tonight Lorna. Don't get me wrong, but it's more than most would have done. But you could have died."

"I wasn't thinking of that at the time."

"Why did you consider saving her? She murdered her husband; most would have said she deserved to die."

"But does that give someone the right to kill two more innocent people? No one even knows yet if she did kill him." I thought about Declan; not only using me to kill his wife, but his nephew and sister-in-law as well. "Maybe she had good reason to kill him."

"Is there ever a good reason to kill someone?" he asked. I wondered about what her life with Declan might have been like, how he'd betrayed her trust, and that in the end it had been an accident.

"Yes." I answered, maybe too quickly. He looked at me suspiciously. The rest of the trip passed in silence. I sat thinking ... about Ben and his mum, how it was my fault they were dead. Had I traded one little boy's life for my brother? I hated Declan so much I struggled to contain my anger. I wanted to hit and smash everything in sight. He'd used me. I felt contaminated. I didn't know what he'd had planned but I was a fool if I'd ever thought he'd leave me unharmed. If he'd not lost control of my mind I'd still be inside that fire. If he'd stayed inside my head for one minute longer I'd have been dead. I wasn't supposed to be alive.

I wanted so badly to hurt him, but he was dead - and I didn't know how to get rid of him. I couldn't help my thoughts wavering over Lynette. Maybe I should have left her for dead. I thought that perhaps he'd stop invading me if she were also dead; maybe killing just one of us would have satisfied him. He wasn't about to leave it at the fire. How many more innocent people would die in his mission to kill his wife? I wanted Bobby safe, and my family, and I wanted my mind back. I was disgusted with myself for thinking it, but ... if I was back in that fire I wasn't sure I'd save her again.

The engine droned to a halt and the paramedic opened the doors. I rose unsteadily to my feet to be helped onto a bed in Accident and Emergency. Two nurses and a doctor hurried in. The paramedic quickly briefed them and left. The nurses cleaned the soot from my skin revealing burns to my back and legs. One rubbed a cool, gel-like substance onto my burns, agonising at first. I recoiled at the cold but felt it soothing my skin. The doctor checked my chest and lungs. Smoke had done some damage but nothing too serious. He still wanted to keep me in overnight - just in case. He declared my burns superficial; a relief. They should heal fully and leave no scarring. After the doctor and nurses had left I went into the toilets to look in the mirror.

I saw my dirty brown hair, burnt, dead. I ran a hand through my hair. Charred bits fell to the floor. The hair had protected my scalp, for which I was grateful; it would grow back and shouldn't look too bad after a wash . Hopefully a hairdresser could chop away the burnt bits. Although the backs of my ankles were blistered and sore, the rest of my feet and legs, surprisingly, weren't that bad. I guess I'd managed to get into the bedroom before the flames had caught up. I was wearing a hospital gown - my pyjamas were falling apart having suffered the worst of the damage. I undid the gown tapes exposing my back. I winced. Angry blisters dotted my skin in obscure patterns. I quickly re-tied the tapes and moved away. I didn't want to look at myself any longer. One of the nurses came back to say that the police would like to speak to me, if I felt ready. I was as ready as I ever would be. She took me to an empty waiting room. I passed Gary on the way and declined his offer to accompany me. One minor deviation from my original story and I'd be caught out, and God knows what I'd do then.

Two male detectives came in. I felt embarrassed, sitting there in a gown, them in suits. Greetings were offered and a recorder was placed on the table and switched on. The officer on the left looked friendly, quite small, about fifty, and approachable. The second officer was tall with large dark eyes and dark hair to match. I guessed him to be in his late twenties, his smile seemed genuine but there was a seriousness about him.

"You don't mind if we use this do you?" The detective had just told me his name, but I'd already forgotten. I shook my head.

"You could always write a statement but it's likely we'll have further questions later on. Besides, I prefer talking over what happened, helps my old brain understand more clearly," the older detective said.

"The tape is okay," I replied.

"I understand this may feel a bit strange, a police interview in a hospital waiting room, but the station is supposed to make you feel intimidated; that's not what I want." They said all the formal stuff at the beginning of the tape and then started questioning me. I told them what I'd told Gary and the paramedic, hoping I was sticking to my original story. It was all done in a friendly manner, no pressing questions, but it still felt like interrogation, especially when every word from my mouth was a downright lie. I discovered they'd already had a quick word with Paul and some other neighbours who hadn't had anything useful to say. They'd seen the same as Gary. The detectives appeared slightly dubious about parts of my story. However, like Gary and the paramedic, decided that I'd no reason to lie. I was after all a witness, not a suspect.

I thought of the petrol canister. They'd eventually find it. If I didn't mention it, it may have looked suspicious. Also, in case my DNA had survived the impossible and was still on the canister I needed to cover my tracks. So, I blurted out, "There was a petrol canister, near the flames. I picked it up and threw it to the back of the kitchen once I'd realized what it was." I spoke fast, hoping I'd given the impression I'd only just remembered. They beamed, knowing I'd confirmed their suspicions.

"Arson," they voiced as one.

"Ruling out all the suspects will be quite a task. She's our prime suspect for the murder of Declan Rhodes," the younger detective said.

"Lorna ... you sure you didn't see anyone?" the elderly detective asked.

"Sure."

"You said you were looking out of the window because you couldn't sleep. Was there anything suspicious that drew your attention to number 4?"

"Flames." I replied.

"Anything else?"

"No."

"Any cars on the street that night that you didn't recognise?"

"No." I don't notice cars. "Do you really think she killed her husband?" I asked.

"Well, we can't be certain, but evidence doesn't usually lie." The younger detective, surprisingly, answered my question.

"What if she'd had no choice? What if it was self-defence, or she hadn't meant to?" Both detective's eyes drilled into mine. *Ooops.* "Lorna, is there something you're not telling us?"

"No." I'd replied much too fast.

"Do I need to remind you how serious this is? It's a murder investigation. Perverting the course of justice can lead to a custodial sentence." I remained silent for a moment, knowing I'd have to reply soon. But what to say?

"I've told you everything I know about the fire. I haven't lied ... this is about Lynette and her husband." I hesitated. I'd have to spill now. Deep down I knew I'd wanted to tell them. What was the point in saving someone's life if they were only going to spend the rest of it behind bars? I just didn't want any more questions.

"Go on." The second detective urged me on. Both knew they were getting more answers from me than they'd hoped for.

"I saw Declan and his mistress together. I took a photo and confronted him. I said I'd tell Lynette, so he destroyed my phone and threatened me."

"But he was going to tell Lynette anyway - he was going to run away."

"He wasn't going to tell her. He was going to kill her." The detectives gaped. I was telling the truth. I knew I was correct. Declan had left behind his thoughts and memories as well as his fears when he'd entered my mind. I hadn't realised it until now.

"He destroyed my phone but not the memory card. I still had the photo of him with the other woman. I mailed the photo to his wife, but he opened the letter." The expressions on their faces were priceless.

"I was walking home from college, he pulled up beside me in his car, blocked my path and told me to get in the car."

"You didn't get in ... ?" The older detective looked appalled.

"I had no choice. He'd got out of the car and grabbed me before I could do anything. He drove us to the woodland park." (It dawned on me I should have lied about that part as well. That's where I'd found his body. My saying so was far too suspect.) "The car park was deserted. At first he just talked." I began my story quickly, before they could connect the two bits of information.

"What did he say?"

"He had a new job in Singapore ... was moving out there with this woman. I spoke to Lynette afterwards; she thought they were just going to Singapore on holiday. They'd told everyone they were going on holiday. He told me, in the car, that he wasn't going to let Lynette have a penny from him, not the house, not the car. He was going to kill her then move to Singapore with his mistress. He'd pretend there'd been an accident abroad and Lynette had died. That way he could sell the house in Britain, keep all of the money and start a new life without Lynette." I didn't know for how long I'd had this information, but that was his plan. I knew I was right.

"Why did he tell you this?" the younger detective asked.

"He didn't think he'd get caught. I only figured out his whole plan after I'd spoken to Lynette. He didn't think I'd do that."

"What did he say that made him so sure you wouldn't tell?"

"It was what he did." I stared at the detectives, hoping they'd understand. I felt uncomfortable talking about it.

"No." The younger detective whispered, as though we shouldn't be talking about it.

"He touched me, he was so close to me. His hands were everywhere and I couldn't get him off. I told him to stop. Eventually he did. He told me that '*this time*' I'd been lucky, next time he wouldn't stop." I couldn't look at the officers. I hadn't told anyone what he'd done. It still revolted me.

"You should have told us ... the police."

"I had no proof. He lived across the road. If you'd let him go then he would have hurt me or worse."

"But you told Lynette ..."

"I didn't want him to get away with it completely. I told her everything. She didn't believe me at first."

"What eventually made her believe you?"

"He admitted it that night. He was going to kill her, but she got in first. If she hadn't, I'd also be dead. He was a monster." I stopped and looked at them, hoping they believed me.

"We'll have to speak to Lynette again. Maybe she'll talk now she knows what Lorna has said. And, if it was self-defense there's no case," the younger detective said.

"We need a team meeting asap. Speak to the judge and the prosecutor. I think everyone will want to concentrate on the arsonist now. The death of a woman and child, rightly or wrongly, gets higher priority."

"Have you told anybody else what you've just told us?"

"No."

"I think it would be best if you told your mum and dad. It's not good to keep such things secret. They'll want to know."

"How is Lynette?" I asked.

"She's not physically harmed, thanks to you. But she's not in a good way." I nodded. I understood. "I think it's best you tell your parents."

"I will."

"Shall I get your dad?" the elderly detective asked.

"Stepdad, but yeah, thanks."

"Interview suspended, 04:23." The detective then went to speak to Gary.

"You did the right thing, telling us. You may well have prevented an innocent women going to jail."

"Some will never believe she's innocent ... she did kill him."

"The law protects us in rare cases such as this. Help is also available for you. I could arrange a councillor or alternative support."

"I'm fine. Anyway, he's dead now, it's over." I wished it was the truth. Gary came in looking worried.

"The officer said you had something to say."

"I'd rather tell you and Mum together. It's nothing to worry about." I'd put him through enough stress for one night. I didn't want to inflict anymore but ... it would be so hard telling them separately, and I didn't fancy doing it twice.

"Is Lorna in trouble?" Gary asked the detectives.

"Not at all."

"We have a busy night ahead and should be off. We'll be in touch." The younger detective smiled at me.

"Thank you for the information. If you remember anything else, or need our help, please give us a call." The older detective handed me a card with his details. I shook both their hands, as did Gary, and they left.

"What information did you have?"

"I'll tell you later. First I need to see if the doctor will let me go home." He wouldn't, even though morning light was only a couple of hours away. Gary phoned Mum. She hadn't gone back to bed and insisted on coming straight down. She asked a neighbour to sit in our house in case Bobby woke up. Gary then got us both drinks and we sat on my bed making small talk. There were no other patients on this part of the ward. I worried over how they'd react. I knew I should have told them at the time and had no reason for not telling. Then I'd found his body in the woods and suddenly it all looked far too suspicious.

"Lorna! Are you okay?" Mum hurried into the ward.

"Yeah, Mum, I'm fine."

"What did the police say? Why did they say you need to talk to us?" I'd already told Gary what the police had asked about the fire and didn't want to repeat everything to Mum.

"They just asked about the fire."

"What did you tell them? You told me you didn't know anything," Gary asked.

"I don't have any information about the fire. It's about Lynette ... and Declan."

"What information?" Mum demanded.

"Lynette killed Declan." They reacted simultaneously. I couldn't understand what they were saying but read the shock on their faces.

"It was an accident, sort of. She did it to stop him from hurting me."

"Why would he want to hurt you?" I sensed they only half-believed me.

"When I was working at the restaurant I saw Declan and his mistress ... together." I'd begun now so couldn't stop. It felt as though I'd waited weeks to tell them. I couldn't look them in the eyes while talking about the woodland park experience. I was uncomfortable talking about his hands on me, and couldn't help thinking that now he had his hands wrapped around my mind ... much, much worse. Thankfully they let me talk without interruption.

"Sick bastard. If he wasn't already dead I'd kill him myself," Gary said.

"That's what you meant in the ambulance, wasn't it?" He sat up straight then, looking at me, though he'd finally understood something. I gave him a puzzled look. He carried on, seeing that I hadn't realized what he was saying.

"When you said that there is sometimes a reason for murder ... you meant him?"

I smiled. "Yes."

"Lorna. Do you ever listen to anything anyone tells you?" Mum snapped. It was the first thing she said, her tone was harsh.

"What do you mean?"

"Do not get into a car with a stranger. Do not enter a burning building. These are basic lessons you learn when you're a toddler. This is what we should be telling Bobby, not you. You're eighteen, what kind of example are you setting for Bobby?"

"Declan wasn't a stranger. I knew him, and I didn't know the house was going to blow up."

"This is not the time for your smart mouth."

"Liz, I know you're upset, but it's not Lorna's fault. She's been very brave, we should be proud of her." I was glad Gary, at least, was on my side.

"Proud? She could have died. She's been a bloody idiot, that's what. God knows what could have happened to her. Everyone's acting like she's a hero ... she's not. She's my daughter and I want her safe." I didn't blame her for being annoyed. She was worried, scared for me. She didn't yet know about the drug gang holding a knife to my throat round at Dad's. I decided no one needed to know about that right then. "Liz, she's okay. Nothing bad has happened to her." Mum stared furiously at Gary.

"Some dirty old man has had his filthy hands on my daughter and '*nothing bad*' has happened?" Mum stood up and walked away. Gary sighed.

"She'll calm down soon." He stood up and went after her. She stayed silent all the way home. Once there she went straight upstairs and started ironing. I stood at my window and watched number 4. The firemen were still there. The flames had been doused but smoke still rose into the air. The house was just a shell, one and a half walls remained. The rest was smouldering rubble. Two jets of water were still being sprayed onto it. No evidence of anything would be found in there, my story would stand. Gary came into my room.

"It's over, Lorna." I wished it was.

"Two people are under there." It was the only thing on my mind.

"Just be glad you aren't one of them." I couldn't.

"What will they look like?" (Stupid question.)

"I don't know. But don't be watching the house all day. You don't want to see the bodies when they come out. It'll only upset you."

"How's Mum?"

"Shaken."

"Yeah." The street looked so different with that one house missing. "Where's Bobby?"

"Next door. They didn't mind having him for an hour. He is, after all, the brother of the hero."

"Don't." It made me feel sick, watching the house, knowing that two people lay buried under there. I didn't feel much like a hero. I saved a murderer's life ... hardly something to be proud of. Gary didn't speak for a while.

"I'll take you to the hairdressers ... if you want?"

"You, take me to the hairdressers?" I laughed.

"Yeah. What's wrong with that?" Gary never noticed when Mum had been to the hairdressers but we got in the car and drove.

"You have to make an appointment. You can't just walk in," I told him.

"Today you can." I looked at him. He smiled mischievously, opened the door for me and we walked to the reception desk.

"Hello, can I make an appointment?" The receptionist looked down at the diary.

"We have a space on Thursday afternoon."

"I'm wanting the appointment now."

"I can't just do that, the next free space is next Thursday."

"But no one is here now."

"I'm sorry, Sir but you'll have to book, like everyone else."

"Have you heard about the fire last night?"

"Yes." The receptionist replied, perplexed.

"Well, you will know that a teenage girl saved the life of the occupant?"

"Yes."

"Well, my step-daughter here is that teenage girl, so could you please get one of your employees to cut her hair?" The receptionist looked at me for the first time and realized he was telling the truth. My cheeks reddened with embarrassment.

"Oh, of course. One minute, Sir." She stood up and walked into the room at the back of the salon. I laughed. Gary smiled. A hairdresser appeared a minute later. She first washed my hair. I looked in the basin when she'd finished. Clumps of my hair were clogging it.

"You had a lot of burnt hair at the back which snapped off as I was washing it," she said, seeing my concern. "Don't worry, we still have a lot to work with." I was actually quite happy when she'd finished. It was a much shorter than I'd ever had, but I'd get used to it. She'd styled the front and my hair fell in line with my jaw. The back was so short it barely touched my neck but it looked so much better than an hour earlier. Gary was near the window looking at hair magazines. I walked over to him.

"Do you think this will suit me?" He pointed to a page in the book, it showed a short-haired, woman's, spikey, punk style cut, dyed black with a pink tinge.

"You should ask the woman to cut it like that for you." We both laughed and went to the counter.

"How much is due?" He asked.

"Nothing, Sir. No charge. Our pleasure."

"You're very kind, thank you." I smiled and walked out of the salon.

"If I'd known that I'd have asked for colour and highlights," I said.

"It looks lovely as it is."

"Thank you." We drove home. Gary made me wait in the car while he fetched Bobby. He came back with a hyperactive toddler.

"Right, where do you want to go kids? I thought we could have a day out somewhere." I realised what he was doing.

"So, you jumped from the window?" Bobby asked, for the fifth time.

"Yeah."

"Wow." His response to my every answer.

"No more questions, Bobby. And remember ... you must never play with fire, it's very dangerous and you mustn't ever jump from a window." Bobby wasn't listening. Gary had known this would happen, which is why he hadn't wanted us inside. Mum would have gone ballistic with Bobby.

"So, where do you want to go?"

"Can we go anywhere?" Bobby asked.

"Yes."

"Cool."

"So, where do you want to go." We settled for the zoo. Not that I was being ungrateful, but I couldn't enjoy it. Gary noticed. I felt guilty for noticing his efforts to help me forget for a while, but I couldn't. I was cold, tired, in pain, and the animals were just animals; I'd seen all before. My attempts at showing interest were half-hearted. On the way home I drifted into an unbroken, dreamless sleep. Arriving home I went straight upstairs and put on a movie, letting my mind wander out of reality into a fictional character adventures and dilemmas.

Fire and police crews stayed until dark. I watched for a long time. The forensics team didn't appear to have discovered anything. I hadn't thought they would. The house was a blackened shell. For hours I lay on my bed reading, wanting to be alone, free from Mum and Gary. Eventually, switching off my light, I settled down under my duvet and waited for Declan to come. I waited ... and waited ... heard Mum and Gary go to bed ... then, stillness and quiet. Still I waited, certain he'd be in my mind at the first opportunity. So, when midnight had come and gone with no sign of him, I felt quite bewildered ... not what I'd expected. Then, on the very brink of sleep, that time of nothingness when thoughts run into dreams, a small irritation disrupted my peace. Once there, it stuck. I grew increasingly uncomfortable by the second.

"*Lorna.*" My name ... whispered, hoarse, on the verge of disappearing: Declan, but not like before. I felt him digging his way ever deeper into my brain. The pain was excruciating. I tossed, turned and thrashed about under the duvet. My efforts to be rid of him frustrated him more than ever. And he was hurting, just like me. I felt it. Unintelligible sounds escaped my lips. I was about to scream out loud. He was fighting. My pain no longer belonged to me. I dived down into his mind, deeper and deeper. It was the only way I could escape.

The light was a brilliant white. Calm and peace floated and swirled in and out of my mind. There was a voice, yet I heard nothing. I had to go on. But first I had to do something. I had to stay – dangerous but no matter. Whispered words of warning sounded like alarm bells in my mind. I ignored them and walked back. The peace dissolved, the sky turned murky. I walked further, clouds on the horizon turned a deeper grey, darkening. I walked towards them. The voice was now roaring, everything going black, thunder echoing - my last chance to turn back. But I wasn't yet ready, not just yet - too soon for me. I'd come back later ... if I could. I took one more step and tripped off the horizon, falling into nothing. Would I be able to get back?

I opened my eyes. I was back on Earth. It felt wrong somehow, as though I shouldn't be. I couldn't walk, instead gliding effortlessly forward, looking down. There I was, lying on the floor. My broken body on the floor. I couldn't bear to look and averted my gaze upwards. There she was - the woman who'd done it to me. My wife. She stands on the top step, higher up than me, how she dares. I charge straight at her - and right on through her. I let out a roar of fury that only I could hear. I could barely believe that she'd ripped me from my body, from my wonderful life now lost forever. But I was still on this Earth. I came back and I'm not leaving without her. I'll steal her life, the way she stole mine. I know how to do it. I know everything. I'm invincible now, no human can kill me. I fly upward out of the house into the starry sky. I see the moon, its pure white glow lighting up the sky. I could fly to it now, go straight through it, and on to the next life. But not yet. I shouldn't be on this world and one newborn could destroy my existence. One newborn on the first full moon of its life could ruin my soul. Its life on this Earth can be exchanged for my spirit. I will not let that happen. I will take her life, and one day soon I'll be flying up through that moon into the unknown. Then I'll be ready.

His ferocity pounded in my head. I'd entered his mind. I'd been him in the first few moments of his death. And now I knew how to get rid of him, not just kill him - destroy him for good. He knew I'd kill him. He couldn't stop me. He was weak, couldn't control me any longer. He'd lost me during the fire, that's why I'd woken up and rescued her. I knew so much about him, why he possessed me, how he did it. The younger the mind the easier to break into. That explained why he'd chosen me. He also wanted to hurt me ... blaming me as much as Lynette for his death. Living so close to the place where he'd died gave him easy access. But I knew he was weak and damaged. He could only possess me while I slept, when my mind was at its most vulnerable, but hadn't the strength to do it for long periods. His spirit was fading. Simply being in my mind now was costing him energy. A baby born on the first full moon ... its life could be traded for the spirit. That's why he'd taken Mum's baby; so that nothing could harm him.

"How'd you do that?" he demanded.
"I just did."
"Why are you still here?"
"I need to make sure you don't do anything stupid."
"Stupid! You made me kill a mother and child. And my Mum's baby died to protect you, not purely so you could blackmail me. And you don't want me doing anything stupid? Killing you would be the best thing I could ever do. "
"I beg you, don't kill me. I can't go through that again."
I laughed. *"If I hadn't broken free of you, would I have escaped from that fire alive?"*
"No." I could read his mind as easily as I could hear my own thoughts.
"Get out of my head!"
"Just promise me you won't try and kill me. I'll move on when I can and leave you alone. I won't hurt you again." Pathetic pleading.
"D'you think I'm stupid? You won't go unless I make you. I've been in your head. You're so dead-set on revenge you won't leave Earth until you've killed Lynette. And you don't care if you take me with her."

"You want to play games, Lorna? Fine. You really think you can beat me? I'm weak now, but not for long. I will make you kill her. I don't care who gets in my way. If I think you're planning something, I'll make your life hell."

"I'm no idiot. You won't be able to do anything for a long time, you're nothing, Declan. You're dead, and I'm going to make sure you stay that way."

"You're wrong, Lorna, you can't win. If you think setting the fire was bad enough, you just wait." A loud noise was pushing us apart. Before I could argue I was wide awake. He was gone. The noise ... ringing a tune. A light shone beside me. Something was vibrating - my phone. I grabbed it from my bedside table. The letters K-A-T-E on the screen. Panic. I answered.

"Kate!" I whispered urgently into the phone.

"I'm so sorry ... didn't know what else to do ... please help ... I have no-one else." She sobbed hysterically down the phone.

"Kate, what's happened?"

"The baby's coming." It took a second or two to register in my head.

"Where are you now?"

"In the B'n B."

"Go to the hospital."

"I can't. Social services will take my baby. They visited me after my arrest. They say I'm not fit to be a mother. But if you're with me I stand a chance. I can't lose my baby. I just need to prove that it's your dad's and we'll be okay. But if I go to the hospital Social Services will be there, and they'll take my baby." She was rushing her words, panicking.

"Kate, calm down. Can you get to my dad's?"

"Yeah, I'll get a taxi."

"Dad's still in America. I'm coming straight up now." I was already out of bed.

"You can't. It's the middle of the night."

"I'll catch a late train. I'll meet you there and we can figure something out, okay? I'm not letting anyone take my brother or sister away."

"No ... please don't ... you'll be in so much trouble."

"It doesn't matter. I'm going to get ready now."

"Don't go. I'm so scared."

"It's going to be fine. Get to my dad's. I'll meet you there. Everything'll be okay ... see you in a few hours. Don't worry."

"Lorna!"

"Bye." I hung up, switched on my bedside lamp, not thinking about what I'd actually said I'd do. It was crazy. I pulled on jeans and a T-shirt, then packed a bag full of clothes and things I might need for a few nights. Slipping trainers on my feet I grabbed a thick jacket, turned off the light and crept out of my room, closing the door carefully. I tiptoed downstairs, not drawing breath, crept into the kitchen and clambered, in the dark, onto one of the work surfaces. Running my hand along the tops of cupboards, I found the old biscuit tin. Feeling extremely guilty I opened it. Inside, lay a small clear bag filled with notes. I stuffed it into my pocket, opened a drawer and took out the back door key. My conscience finally caught up with me. I scribbled a note for Mum and Gary.

So sorry, have to go somewhere. Will be back soon, you will get the money back, I promise. I'm fine, please don't worry.
Love Lorna xx

I felt more guilty. They deserved more than a tacky little note. But there was no time - Kate needed me more. About to walk out the door I remembered something. I went back and grabbed a torch from the drawer. It would be pitch black at dad's. I closed and locked the back door behind me, climbed over the gate and walked out to the street. I gently patted my blistered hands on my jeans. The rough, peeling paint on the gate had scratched my already injured hands. I looked up, trying to figure out a plan of action. Wispy clouds could be seen drifting across the nearly full moon, a spectacular sight. Stars twinkled in the night sky. The longer I stared the more bright tiny lights appeared. But I couldn't stargaze for long ... had to get moving. I zipped my jacket all the way up in an attempt to cease my chattering teeth. With the torch in one jacket pocket I checked I had the money and my phone. It was about half-past midnight. Last time the train to dad's had taken about four hours. Hopefully Kate could hold on.

Chapter 9

I headed for the bars and takeaways. There'd be taxis at this time of night to catch to the train station. I walked quickly and was soon in the centre of town. I managed to avoid the drunks and groups of teenagers who should have been in bed.

"The train station please." The driver looked at me suspiciously. My casual clothes told him I hadn't been on a night out, and I probably didn't look old enough to be out. He said nothing and drove me to the station. Rap music was blaring from the radio so we didn't speak.

"£4.44 please." I handed him the money.

"Thank you, good night."

"Good night." I climbed out of the warm car into the cold night. The rap music faded away as I headed for the empty platform, lit by one small lamp. I sat shivering on a bench. A few raindrops fell on me. Bushes grew all alongside the track. I studied the timetable; the last train of the night to the main city station was due shortly. It seemed like hours waiting as the rain fell even heavier. I was soon soaked, feeling like I was in a scene from some tragic movie. It was such a relief when I heard the train approaching. Its headlight shone around the corner and it slowed on reaching the platform - only two carriages. I stood up and leapt on board the moment the doors opened, worried they'd close if no one was seen getting off. A young couple and three men sat dotted around the carriage. I sat on the seat nearest the door, huddling low, but already every eye was on me. I felt sick. They'd all be wondering *'who was this kid'*, all alone in the middle of the night, visibly cold and very wet. I felt uncomfortable and kept my eyes down, carefully studying my cold hands already purple from the cold, my palms still red and blistered from my burns. I looked at no one. The ticket man approached me. I told him where I was going and paid. Two more people boarded over the next couple of stops and everyone climbed out at the main station. In the station toilets I splashed some water on my face to freshen up. Looking in the mirror for the first time I understood why I'd got so many questioning glances. My newly cut hair was wet and looked a mess. My jacket hadn't concealed the angry red burns to the back of my neck and my eyes had dark bags under them. I looked about fifteen years old but I didn't suppose it mattered. I combed my fingers through my hair so it fell where it should. I didn't look good, but certainly much improved.

The train timetables were so confusing but I eventually worked out I needed to be on platform 3. It took a while to find as it was nowhere near 1 or 2, which I thought was a bit stupid. The directions took me over numerous bridges and I found myself at the station exit, back at platform 7 where I'd started. After much searching and walking around in circles I found platform 3. I stood away from other passengers waiting for the train. It amazed me the number of people in the station, all rushing around in the small hours. In a few hours' time Mum would be getting up with Bobby and find me gone. I pushed the guilt away as I thought of Kate, alone, scared and in pain. The train pulled in. I sat at the back in the last carriage, feeling out of place. Nobody seemed to notice. There were all sorts of different people on the train, business men, people going on holiday, even a couple of toddlers with their parents. One child was asleep on its father's shoulder. I was glad once we were on our way. I felt a lot calmer knowing I was safely on my journey ... hundreds of miles across country. Kate phoned.

"Lorna?"

"Kate, are you okay?"

"I'm scared."

"It's going to be okay, I'm on my way. Where are you now?"

"I'm outside the gate. The taxi has just dropped me off. I need the code." For a second it crossed my mind this could be a set-up. She might not be alone, might be with those men again. If I gave her the code they could burgle the house again. However, I didn't think the fear in her voice could be so well faked.

"5286." If she betrayed my trust again I'd be in big trouble.

"It's not working."

"Try again. 5286."

"No. It's not right. You sure it's the right code?"

"Yeah, I'm certain. Cancel it and try again."

"It's still not working." Panic was creeping into her voice.

"Are you sure you're pressing the right numbers?"

"Yes! I'm using my phone to light up the keypad."

"I've got the code typed on my phone, hold for a second." I checked the notepad on my phone, 5286 appeared on my screen. I went back to the call. "5286 is definitely right."

"And I'm telling you it's not working." Kate replied, adamant.

"Dad must have changed it after the break-in. " It was the only explanation that made sense.

"Oh shit!"

"Kate, you're going to have to go to the hospital. I'll be with you in a couple of hours, I promise."

"No way! I know another way in. There's a fence around most of the property, but I can get in through the woods, the way I did the first time I met you." I was not happy with the idea.

"Dad says the woodland is hundreds of metres thick. You'll need to walk for ages all the way around the fence just to get to the start of the woods."

"I've done it before."

"Kate, it's pitch black outside."

"I'm not scared of the dark!"

"Kate, please don't. It's dangerous." I hated the woods. During my last moonlight wander Declan had taken me to the woodland - I'd found his body. I couldn't imagine doing that while in labour.

"It's fine, practically a straight line through. I'll be able to open the gate from the inside by the time you get here. You have the key to the house and then we go inside and everything will be okay."

"Please ... just go to the hospital!"

"I can't! I can't do that, you know I can't. I won't let them take my baby." I knew there was no point arguing.

"How are you feeling now? You think you're up to the walk?"

"I think so. Labour can take days, I'll be okay. Baby will just have to wait until its big sis is here."

"Phone me if you need anything."

"I will."

"Bye Kate."

"Bye Lorna. See you soon." She was crazy! Out of her mind. I wished the train would go faster, aware that with each passing minute her condition could be deteriorating. I needed to get to her quickly and persuade her to go to the hospital. I knew she'd go if I went with her.

I'd tried keeping my voice down throughout the conversation even though the carriage was silent, except for the rumble over the tracks. I stared out of the window for most of the journey, my mind a roller-coaster of emotions, nothing but my own thoughts for company. The other passengers were either asleep or listening to music. Even the ticket collector looked like he'd rather have been in bed. I was still wide awake despite the hour. I gripped my phone tightly but heard no more from Kate - a positive sign. She'd have phoned if something was wrong. The train eventually arrived at my station. I was glad to have made it. But once out on the empty platform I felt sick with anxiety. I stepped away from the tracks, gathering my breath, searching for an exit. The station was similar to the last, only much quieter. A couple of dim bulbs the only light. It would be bustling in a few hours' time.

Everyone at home would still be asleep with no idea I was halfway across the country. The thought was both thrilling and nauseating. I scanned the timetables but the next train to the town near Dad's wasn't until 7:15am. Kate couldn't wait outside in the cold that long. My plan now looked rather thoughtless. How would I get to Dad's from the next station? I should have known that smaller train lines wouldn't run right through the night. I had only a vague idea of where I was and not a clue how to get to where I wanted to be. A sign pointed to the exit. I followed it and noticed posters and cards advertising local businesses stuck onto the brickwork. One of them advertised a twenty-four-hour taxi service. I stopped and stared at it for a moment, grinning ... exactly what I needed. I took out my phone. After a few rings a lazy male voice answered.

"Cooper's cabs. How can I help?"

"I'd like to order a taxi." I told him where I was.

"Where you going?" I dwelt on my answer for a moment ... I didn't even know Dad's address. I told him the town near Dad's instead.

"Got an address?"

"I don't know exactly, it's about a fifteen minute drive from the train station, but I know the way."

"Someone'll be there in five."

I walked out of the station and waited on the semi-lit street. The rain had slowed to a drizzle and the wind had calmed but the night air was still bitter with a light fog. I prayed Kate would be okay and that it hadn't rained. Buildings towered over me. All I could hear was my own breathing. After a few minutes of anxious waiting the taxi pulled up. I got in the front seat – reluctantly. I would rather have sat in the back, but I needed to see where I was going so I could direct the driver.

The drive was longer than I'd expected; it was going to be a pricey trip. I'd hoped I wouldn't need to spend all the money I'd taken, but now ...? What made it worse was the awful music blasting from the radio, although it meant I didn't have to talk and there were no awkward questions. I reminded myself that the volume was that high to keep the driver awake. He kept gulping from an energy drink, clearly tired, whereas I was still wide awake and getting fidgety. I just wanted to be with Kate. As we left the main road I directed him. There was no need to go into the town itself. I surprised myself at how well I'd remembered directions, especially in the dark. The fog was thickening. The lack of street lights made it tough to see more than immediately ahead. We reached a junction and thankfully I recognised it.

"Left here." The bus stop was around the next corner and I knew the lane to Dad's would be on my left.

"There'll be a lane on the left somewhere along here." He nodded. The headlights lit up a small clearing on the left and he quickly swerved into it, narrowly avoiding a few hundred-year-old trees.

"Just here." The driver looked at me, confused.

"The house is just down the lane but there's no room to turn around."

"Are you sure you don't want me to go any further?"

"I'm sure."

"£65.00 please." I tried not to appear shocked, knowing it meant I'd pretty much spent all Mum and Gary's emergency money. I took the money from my coat pocket and handed it to him, climbed out of the car, grabbed my bag and closed the door. Headlights from the car lit up a small path for me until he'd reversed and turned back onto the road. Then I was left to walk up the lane in darkness. I switched on my torch, lighting up two or three metres ahead of me. Other than that I remained in darkness so dark the fog made no difference to my vision. I walked on up the lane trying to convince myself that goosebumps were from the cold only. I took out my phone - one bar of signal - hope-fully enough. I dialled Kate. An automated voice ... '*this number cannot be reached.*' My blood froze. I tried again ... '*this number cannot be reached*'

... the same voice. I rushed up the lane. The gate was shut. I typed in the code. A small red light flashed once and that was it, no click to indicate it had opened. I pushed on the black iron bars but they weren't moving. I tried the code again. The same red light. I cursed aloud. I pushed and rattled the bars but they didn't budge. There was no way I could climb over. The bars were round and sleek, slippery with rain. "Kate!" I yelled.
"KATE!" I shouted louder, to seemingly empty woods.

She obviously hadn't made it. I couldn't phone her. It'd been hours since I'd last spoken to her. Anything could have happened. I sprinted hard up the drive, ignoring the looming trees and my breathlessness. My heart was pounding as I reached the country lane. I walked to my right, across a field towards the woods. In the fog it was impossible to see individual trees but their dark wall looming in the distance was visible. The field seemed to darken as I drew closer the woods. The circle of my torch beam appeared to be shrinking, closing in. The smooth ground of carefully ploughed fields changed to rough, natural forest floor, the first tree appearing several metres ahead of me. There would be many more concealed in the fog. I stood at the forest fringe. Unlike the previous occasion when I'd wandered around the woods at night, this was very much a voluntary decision to scare myself stupid. My heart would pound, every breath would hang in the air, every leaf crunching underfoot would make me jump. Despite this, I crept behind the tree and on into the live wood.

I'd told myself it was an adventure and forced myself to feel a nervous excitement, trying to stay focused on Kate, on how scared she'd be. I had no choice but to help her. She was the reason I was doing this. As I walked deeper into the woods however, my ability to control my thoughts disappeared ... along with the light ... and my sanity. The trees stood taller and closer together, the ground became rougher, branches wilder. Cries of pain escaped my lips every so often as branches scratched at my face, pulled my hair, scraped my shins. I'd never find her. She might already be at the hospital, but basic common sense told me she'd never have been able to fight her way through this.

I'd tried looking for signs of her, but she could've been anywhere. I tried walking in a straight line but the woods were so wild and some parts too crowded and treacherous to walk through. I just had to keep my eyes and ears open, and concentrate on finding her. But, bloody hell I'd never been so terrified. Again and again I changed direction. Valuable time slipped away. How long had I been in here? I called out her name repeatedly, terrified of attracting unwanted attention from animals possibly living in these woods. I scoured every inch of my small light bubble for any sign that might lead me to her. I walked in what felt like endless circles, pushing branches from my face, continually being ripped to shreds. The pain of the branches scraping my burns was agonising. At no point did the vice-like fear gripping my chest loosen. I heard animals rustling the leaves around me and bugs, attracted by the light, bumbled around my face. And then I heard a cry … a baby!

Of all the signs I'd looked for, this was the sweetest. My heart leapt as I ran towards the sound. I knew she must have been close so I shouted her name. Getting no reply I pushed terrible pictures of her possible fate from my mind. I shone my torch on the ground, found the path she'd taken and followed it. She'd taken the easiest path ... where vegetation spread the furthest apart. Visible clues …   branches she'd snapped and the ground she'd trampled made searching easier. The torch began dimming. I had to squint to see anything beyond a metre ahead. The further I went, the more intensely I scanned the surroundings. The cry was louder so I knew they must be close. I inched forward, determined not to miss her.
"Kate." I called her name a few times. Still no answer, but she was somewhere nearby. The baby had stopped crying. My torch dimmed further. I shone the light to my left and around the next tree to my right. I needed to find them, fast. I backtracked slightly and began another route.

A figure lay sprawled at the bottom of a tree trunk. Another step forward and I found myself standing over Kate's seemingly lifeless body. I dropped to my knees and scanned my torch over her. Her head rested against the tree-trunk, eyes closed, mouth slightly open ... she could have been asleep. I prayed she was. The baby cried. She'd wrapped it in her jacket, her bare arm wrapped protectively around it. I picked up the baby (my brother or sister) and it quietened. Kate's arm fell to her side, but she didn't stir. I pressed two trembling fingers against her neck. She was cold, but warmer than the night air … a very weak pulse. She hadn't gone yet. Her hands were covered in dried blood. I felt congealing blood in which she was lying on my hands. I looked down at the baby and wiped its forehead. I wanted to know if I had a brother or sister but didn't want to unwrap the jacket and expose it to the cold night. Big eyes stared up at me. My heart melted. I held it in one arm against my chest as I tried waking Kate.

"Kate. It's me." I put the torch down and shook her gently. No response. I pulled her head and neck off the tree trunk into a semi-sitting posture hoping it might wake her. No joy. With one arm I could only support her for a few seconds. I laid her back down. She needed medical help, urgently. I didn't have a clue what to do. I took the phone out of my pocket, no signal, but still I dialled 999. A sharp buzz then a message flashed up on my screen … 'no network connection' … as I'd expected. Fear dug a bit deeper. The only way I could help her was by getting out of here. I unzipped my jacket and slipped one arm out. I placed the baby in my other arm and took the jacket off. The cold bit my bare arms instantly. Kate needed the jacket more. I spread it over her, tucking it under her and up to her neck. She felt so cold. Lying on damp ground would not be good for her.

"I'll be back soon with help. I promise." I whispered. A tear ran down my cheek. I couldn't believe I was leaving her but I couldn't carry her, especially not through the woods, and definitely not with a baby. I picked up the torch and put her bag over my shoulder (I knew it held baby things).

"I'm so sorry." I said and kissed baby's forehead then headed back out into the woods. The torch light by now just a pale yellow glow. I could barely see. I forged on, pushing branches from my face, protecting the baby's face with my arms. I had no idea what direction I was walking in. I just hoped it took us out of the woods. The torch flickered then faded. I switched it off and back on. The light blinked on and off for a few seconds, then all was black. Nothing. Everything was dark. I dropped the useless torch on the ground and stood there in the dark, blind and scared. I held baby closer, hearing it breathe and ran my thumb over its warm cheek, happy it was warm and still okay. Taking a deep breath I pressed on. The impossibility of my task dawned on me; I had no chance of finding my way out, especially while carrying a baby.

After a few minutes my eyes adjusted to the dark, enough to make out the trees and branches up ahead but only by their differing shades of black. I couldn't waste any more time. Progress was horribly difficult. My right arm grew heavy and numb from holding the baby. Branches grew thicker forcing me to backtrack several times. Unable to see properly my hearing sharpened, picking up every animal rustle and owl hoot. My footsteps sounded louder. Without my jacket I was cold. The burns on my neck and arms were exposed to sharp, prickly branches. I was in so much pain, and emotionally in a mess. I tucked the baby's head into my chest and made sure it was still wrapped up tight in Kate's coat. My fear and pain were now irrelevant; what mattered was getting out and getting Kate and the baby to hospital. I charged through the branches, my left hand shielding the baby's head. My face took the worst of the scratches. The dark no longer bothered me. The trees eventually thinned out and I finally stood at the edge of the forest.

"We did it," I whispered to the baby, "I thought we'd never get out of there." I looked back at the forest, spread out as far as my eyes could see. "How are we ever going to find mummy again?" Fog swirled above the treeline and I saw mist filling the fields.

I walked on into the mist. When I next looked over my shoulder the woods had disappeared - not a tree in sight, as though I'd walked through a cloud. I picked up my pace. I knew I was on Dad's land; I'd made it through to the other side. Had I come out of the woods on the side I'd entered I'd have reached the country lane by now. The trek was all uphill. That was good. I knew his land sloped down to the woods.

The house loomed through the fog. I rushed up to it with a smile. I found the house key in my bag. Opening the door was the greatest relief in the world. All the tension of the night lifted as I stepped inside. Turning on the hallway light I walked through to the living room and laid the baby on the rug in the middle of the floor then emptied the contents of Kate's bag: a couple of cream babygros, a baby bottle and a soft teddy toy among the contents. I unwrapped the baby from the coat - I had a baby brother! Bobby would be so excited. After cleaning him I dressed him in a babygro. He looked so small but filled the babygro well - a good sign. I picked him up again - didn't want to leave him on the floor, and walked through to the study, its door still slightly ajar from the break-in. I couldn't believe it had happened only a week ago. I opened the door, walked in and began searching through the papers I'd previously stacked on the desk. I needed his address before calling an ambulance. The papers were mostly printed emails but eventually I found some invoices from the building company that I assumed had built the house. The address was printed on the paper. My phone was out of my pocket the minute I saw it. Out of the woods and on higher ground I had a signal. I dialled 999.

"999. What service do you require?"

"Ambulance."

"What is the address of the incident?" I read out the address on the invoice.

"What is the emergency?"

"My Dad's girlfriend has given birth in the woods near my house. She's unconscious and lost a lot of blood. I've got the baby with me now. He seems okay - breathing and inside the house with me now."

"An ambulance is on its way. I'll stay on the phone and ask some questions until the ambulance arrives."

"Okay." I tried sounding calm.

"Is your dad with you?"

"No, he's in America."

"Is anyone else with you?"

"No."

"Are you with your dad's girlfriend now?"

"No. I couldn't carry her and the baby and there was no signal in the woods. I needed to get home to call for help."

"Were you with her during the birth?"

"No. She was trying to reach my dad's house ... it's gated and he must have changed the code since I was last here because there was a burglary. She went through the woods to get to the house. I was going to meet her here, but she didn't make it. I found her lying unconscious but the baby was crying. He's warm now."

"How old are you?"

"Eighteen." She asked endless questions. I answered truthfully. Whether or not she believed me ...? She just wanted to keep me talking, it was her job. All the while I was restless, pacing up and down, baby in one arm, phone in the other. I kept checking to see if the ambulance had arrived - I'd left the gates open. It felt like forever. Finally, the faint hum of sirens growing louder and blue lights flashing through the trees. "They're here." I said *'thanks, goodbye'*, hung up and ran out to greet it, baby brother still in my arms. The sirens stopped. Two paramedics jumped out and came straight over to us. The baby started crying.

"Sounds as though he's got a pair of healthy lungs on him."

"I think he's okay."

"We'll get him checked out at hospital."

"I'm right in thinking you're not the mother?" one of them asked.

"Yeah, his mum is in the woods." I pointed down the hill to the forest. Above the treeline the sky was the boldest blue, a dark and enchanting colour. Overhead the sky had changed to a stunning purple, the sun rising and the fog dissipating.

"Do you know where in there?" The vast treeline looked daunting.

"No. It was pitch dark and it felt like I was in there for hours. I only found Kate because the baby was crying." The paramedic didn't look happy.

"I'm phoning for back up – police and rescue. If we have any chance of finding her alive we need more than just me searching. You said she was unconscious?"

"Yes. There was a lot of blood, but she was definitely alive." The paramedic nodded, went into the ambulance and took out a large green rucksack which he slung on his back.

"You take the baby to hospital, he needs to get checked out." The paramedic addressed his colleague.

I sat in the back of the ambulance, baby on my lap. I looked out across the woods and as the doors closed, silently apologised to Kate. Guilt weighed down on me. I should have stayed to help find her but the thought of going back terrified me; I couldn't bear to find her dead. She'd want me to be with her baby and not let strangers take him away.

I kissed his forehead, rocking him gently. The journey to hospital was short. On arrival a nurse took my brother from me, another led me down a different corridor and sat me on a hospital bed then drew the curtains.

"I'll be back in five minutes," she said. She was gone far longer and I was impatient. I couldn't see anyone through the old, faded blue curtains and felt lost and alone, miles from home. A different nurse came back. She cleaned the scrapes on my face and arms. It stung like hell. I could see her wondering how I'd got my burns on a cold night in the woods.

"I was in a fire."

"How awful, what caused that?"

"Arson."

"When?"

"Last night." It was weird. 24 hours earlier I'd been in a hospital just like this, being cleaned up in the same way, but for completely different injuries.

"You really should have covered your burns more appropriately before going in the woods."

"I had a coat on but I wrapped it around Kate when I went for help." She didn't seem happy with my answer but let it lie.

"I'm finished now but I'll dress the worst burns. The branches have broken through some of the burnt skin. The last thing we need is infection. Take the dressing off in a couple of days. If you feel it needs replacing go to your local health centre." I was made to sit in a waiting room while my brother was being assessed. I hoped that 'assessed' meant medically, and not by the social services. If social services took him I'd have failed Kate. Only 24 hours had passed and I felt as though I was living a different life. I sat down opposite a poster displaying the risks of smoking. I stood up again. Sitting made me feel useless. I paced around the room. Walking helped me feel I had somewhere to go. I switched off my phone. (Not supposed to have your mobile on in hospital.) I didn't bother switching Kate's off (it was in her bag, with me) because I knew no one was going to ring her. The clock ticked away, the noise driving me nuts.

06:37, the note I'd left Mum seemed pathetic. 06:41, guilt was tightening my airways, making me feel sick. 06:44, had Bobby woken up yet? Had they discovered I was gone? 06:49, how long does it take to assess a baby? Had they found Kate?

I paced up and down. The ticking of the clock seemed to hasten time away. I thought of texting Mum and Gary then immediately decided not to; it would be worse than a note. I dumped the option of phoning from outside. What if the nurse came back with news about Kate and I wasn't here? That was my reasoning anyway. They'd go ballistic if I phoned them and couldn't disclose the truth over the phone. They'd make me come home. I needed to stay and help Kate.

Seven o' clock came and went. They'd know I was missing. Seven minutes past seven - they'd have searched the house. Gary would be getting into the car, going out to look for me. The note would have been found. Mum would be sobbing. Bobby too, though he wouldn't understand. He'd know I was missing. Tears welled in my eyes as I imagined his little face, screwed up in confusion, asking for me. Still I didn't turn on my phone. I only needed to phone, tell them I was fine, okay and let them hear my voice. But I'd never be able to hang up, and ... bloody hell ... the trouble I'd be in! Kate needed me and that was that. I'd phone later. It wasn't like I'd *run away* for good. They could even come and pick me up. I'd tell them where I was, everything. Just ... not yet. Once Kate and the baby were safe at home I'd need to tell Dad. How would he react? He couldn't just abandon his child. And then I remembered - he'd abandoned Bobby. This was a terrible situation. I figured Mum would be mad. I'd be lucky to get away unscathed with Dad once he found out I was in contact with Kate. I was in for it.

I had my back to the door. It creaked. I whipped around, stared and froze. Her eyes met mine as she walked into the room. The look on her face scared me back to reality. She didn't have to say a word. I held my breath.
"If you would take a seat ..." Not a question, more of a command, but sounding like she'd asked. Her voice was soft. I obeyed without thinking. She sat down beside me. I felt uncomfortable.
"I'm so sorry, it's not good news." My mouth went dry, my throat

turned into sandpaper. I couldn't find words, even if I could have spoken.

"A body has been found in the woods near your house." I'd prepared myself for this, known it the moment she'd walked in. I still couldn't believe what she'd said. I didn't move a muscle, couldn't breathe, the moment hung. She spoke again.

"Dozens of police and fire officers were called out. They traced every inch of the woods. When they found her, there was nothing anyone could do. They've brought her body back to the hospital." I nodded, numb, unable to speak.

"Her son is perfectly healthy. He's feeding well and his body temperature is normal. You should be proud of yourself." I didn't know how to respond. I tried smiling. No good. My little brother would grow up without a mother. I didn't know how to handle it, torn between grief, and elation at the birth of my brother.

"Would you like to see him?" I nodded ever so slightly. She stood up and I found myself following out the door into the busy passage. People were rushing around but I heard nothing. I followed her along corridors and up stairs. Kate couldn't just be *'gone'*. We'd talked on the phone just hours earlier. She had a baby boy who needed her. I didn't know what to do. Before I could think any further the nurse had ushered me into the baby ward, dimly lit with blue light, no windows and blacked out doors. It was quite big ... several plastic cribs. I followed the nurse towards one and saw a tiny figure moving around inside. She nodded. I went and stood beside the crib. Once again my heart swelled with the love for this so tiny, so beautiful child.

"You can hold him if you want." I looked down. Kate's little boy. I picked him up carefully, thinking no one else in the world knew about him. He felt warm. I cradled him as he searched my face. I don't know if it was possible for him to recognize me, but I think he did. Tears streamed down my cheeks. It was my saddest yet most joyful moment ever. He was so tiny, little arms waving about, tiny fingers grasping at air. A tear spilled onto his cheek. He blinked, startled. I laughed a little. I wiped the tear away, his cheek felt so smooth. I saw a few wisps of dark hair. He looked so beautiful.

"Is there anyone you want us to contact?"

107

"No. There isn't anybody." Kate had no-one.

"Kate's parents?"

"She didn't speak to them but if you find them on your system you can tell them." I presumed they needed to know.

"What about your Dad?"

"He's in America. I'll phone him soon. I think it's best coming from me." I fought to keep my voice steady.

"The police will want to speak to someone, ask questions about Kate."

"Why?"

"There's an investigation after every death. Although she was pregnant, young women don't die for no reason."

"I don't know much, but I'll be able to tell them a few things. Dad will know more."

"That would be appreciated. The body will need to be formally identified."

"Will I have to do that?"

"It's normally a relative."

"I'm the only person she had left. I don't know who else there is." I felt I needed to say goodbye, to tell her I'd look after her son, to say sorry, sorry I'd let her die alone.

"Okay. When you're ready I'll get someone to take you down."

The walls turned a darker shade of grey and the air grew colder as I reached the morgue. Goosebumps on my arms, probably brought on by the atmosphere rather than the chill. The receptionist led me to the small room where Kate's body was being held. I looked down and took a deep breath. A white sheet covered her body. Her arms had been folded, crossed, like she was asleep. Her neck and head lay on a pillow, eyes closed. She'd been cleaned up but scratches still showed on her arms and face. She didn't look like Kate. I'd never before seen her look so peaceful. All her worries - washed away in death.

"It's Kate."

The receptionist nodded and left the room. I felt ashamed at feeling squeamish but I didn't want to touch her. I didn't know if I should have ... guilt?

"You've got a beautiful baby boy," I whispered. "He's healthy. I hope you knew that. I'm glad you got to see him and hold him." I wiped my eyes and stayed silent for a few moments. "I'm really sorry Kate. I promise, I tried to help." I wiped away more tears. I had so many thoughts yet didn't know what to say. She couldn't hear me, couldn't reply. I felt stupid for talking but I couldn't walk away, not just then.

"I'm sorry I left you. I'm sorry I took your son away, I was trying to help. You must have been so scared and I'm sorry I didn't get there sooner. I'm going to look after him. Don't worry about Dad, he'll come round. I promise, Dad will love his son. I'll make sure of that. I'm not going to let anyone take him away from his family. I wish we'd spoken more. I wish I knew what you wanted to call him. Thank you for trusting me. Thank you for letting me try and help, I won't let you down. My brother is going to be a very loved little boy." I touched her hand with the tips of my fingers. She was cold. "You don't have to worry anymore. You can rest now. Move on and please don't come back and haunt me." I chuckled and squeezed her hand. "Goodbye Kate." I took one last, long look at her and backed out the door.

I walked briskly down the corridors, up stairs and eventually I was outside. The morning was bright and crisp, staff were changing shifts, people were rushing. I took little notice and headed for a couple of taxis close by. I still had a little money in my pocket.

Chapter 10

I took a taxi into town and emptied my savings account. A couple of hours later I was back at the hospital. I walked through the automatic doors with a baby car seat in my right hand. I followed the signs to the maternity ward, my head up, walking purposefully, and hopefully masking my anxiety. I strode up to the reception desk. A different woman, maybe in her mid-fifties, sat at the desk, immersed in paper work.

"Hello."

She glanced up.

"A baby boy was brought in today. His mother passed away. I'm the baby's sister." Her bored expression changed. She looked at me with sad eyes. I almost let my front collapse.

"I'm so sorry. I'll get a midwife." She smiled and disappeared into a room behind. I combed my fringe with my fingers and fluffed up my hair with my hand. A midwife came around the corner.

"You must be Lorna?"

"Yes."

"The earlier midwife has updated me on the situation. It must be very difficult. She was worried about you."

"I'm okay. How's the baby?"

"Very well. Let's go see him." The same room as earlier, a bit more brightly lit than before, and there in the same place was Kate's beautiful baby boy. I almost skipped over to him; he was fast asleep.

"Pick him up, it's okay, he'll probably stay asleep." She was right, he barely stirred as I manoeuvred my arms underneath him to support him against my chest.

"Would you care to come into our office? There are some things we need to chat about." We went back down the corridor and into an office unlike any office I'd seen before. There was a desk, chairs and filing cabinets but the pictures on the walls were all of newborn babies, some with parents or siblings, some without. Cuddly toys lay everywhere and the wallpaper had teddy bears on. I sat down on a chair, still holding the baby. He slept on. The midwife had placed the car seat on the chair next to me.

"Put him in there if you want," she said, patting the car seat. I carefully placed him into the seat and adjusted the straps to secure him in place. "Perfect." She smiled. "I've got a bit of paperwork to fill out first. Bear with me, I haven't dealt with a situation like this before. Please give me your name, age and relationship to the child."

"Lorna Cartright, eighteen, and I'm his sister."

"And your address." I gave her Dad's address.

"You and baby share the same father but not the same mother?"

"Yes."

"Where is your father?"

"He's on the first flight back from America." A lie. I had tried calling him but he hadn't answered. He knew nothing and I couldn't just text him the news.

"He was in America to work?"

"Yes. He works mainly in the UK but the company is international." I didn't really know what he did or what company he worked for, or even if he did mainly work in the UK.

"So close to the birth of his child?"

"Dad and Kate weren't getting on. She had a troubled past. As you know, she didn't attend any hospitals during pregnancy. She was scared someone would alert social services; that's why she wouldn't go to the hospital without me last night. Because she didn't go to hospital, no one knew her due date. I don't think she realised it would be so soon."

"Why was she worried about social services?"

"Because of her past; she was technically homeless. I tried helping her as much as I could but I've been living with my Mum hundreds of miles away. She'd allowed a gang of armed robbers to burgle Dad's house a week ago. I was in the house at the time and I pressed charges against her." I was trying to get her to understand the situation. As much as I blamed Dad I didn't want her to know that. I didn't want social services to take the baby away.

"Gosh. This has been a very difficult time for you."

"I'm okay. Last night I was the only person Kate had left. I'd promised to help her, that I wouldn't let anyone take my brother away."

"It's a very difficult situation. In cases such as this the father, or grandparent, normally assumes legal responsibility."

"Kate didn't want her parents involved, they didn't care about her. Dad will be home shortly. The nursery is prepared." She didn't need to know I'd only had time to buy the basics: everything else I'd ordered in town for next day delivery.

"You're eighteen, and a student?"

"Yes." I should have been in college at the time. "But I have a three year old brother. I know how to look after little ones."

"So, you are willing to accept legal responsibility for the child until your father is present?"

"Yes." This is what I was here for, why I'd bought smarter clothes, put on a confident front. I needed her to believe I was capable of looking after the baby, if only for a few days. She looked at me. I only smiled. "Okay. I'll send a midwife to conduct a home visit tomorrow to make sure everything's in order. Someone will need to see your Dad within the week, preferably as soon as he arrives home. There will be much that needs sorting out."

"Okay."

She kept me for a further hour, gathering information on everything from birth certificates to how much I should feed him. She answered any question I could think of. I lost count of how many times I told myself I was being ridiculous. I couldn't look after a baby! I should have told her the truth; that Dad knew nothing about the baby and probably wouldn't care, that I wasn't capable of looking after a baby until he did decide to come home. I didn't. I let her tell me everything I needed to know ... how to look after my brother. She gave me the NHS number so I could call if there were any problems. Next thing I knew we'd finished. I had a bag full of booklets over my shoulder and a car seat with a baby still fast asleep.

"Does he have a name?" I had no right to pick a name.

"Ben." I couldn't stop myself.

"Beautiful. It suits him perfectly." She opened the door and led me down the corridor.

"Take care then, someone will be around tomorrow. Any problems ... you bring him straight back in to us."

"Okay." She'd already disappeared around the corner. My stomach churned. How had this happened? I stood for a moment holding Ben in his car seat, feeling lost. I found my feet and began walking. It felt like I was kidnapping the baby. No one was stopping me from leaving … why? I didn't know how to look after a baby. I'd called him Ben. Why? My '*front*' had shattered, but it had worked. I'd applied make up, styled my hair and bought smart clothes to make me look respectable, trustworthy and mature, but now I wished people could see the child inside and not allow me to take Ben out of the hospital.

The automatic doors opened. I walked out. Blue sky. I couldn't believe I was actually taking him home, just me, alone. Walking towards the taxis I felt sure someone would stop me. Nope. I opened the back door of the nearest taxi and gave the driver Dad's address.

"Aww, isn't he lovely. Congratulations!"

"He's not mine!" I exclaimed. The driver stared at me. "Sorry. He's my baby brother. His mum died … giving birth."

"Oh, I'm so sorry. D'you want any help fastening him in?"

"No, I'll manage." I opened the back door and fastened the car seat in place, then went around to the other side and sat next to Ben in the back.

"Was your mother ill?" The driver asked.

"Not my mum. My dad's ex-girlfriend."

"Where's your dad?"

"In America, working; coming home tonight."

"He went to America when his son was about to be born!" He was shocked, and rightly so.

"He didn't know the due date. It's complicated." Complicated was one way of putting it.

"You had a busy day …?" I asked. Small talk flowed quite comfortably after that. He spoke about work, his '*missus*'. I needed someone to talk to about nothing much at all. The driver didn't pry. He clearly understood it would be the last thing I'd want to talk about, especially to a stranger. He spoke the whole time, told me recent gossip he'd heard as a taxi driver, and commented on Ben - he'd slept through the whole journey.

"Just here on the left." I'd pinned the gates into the ground when the ambulance had come. I never wanted to go back into those woods.

"Wow!" The driver gaped in awe. He drove through the gates onto the large cream stone drive. "I didn't know this was here."

"It hasn't been here long," I said. "Dad built it." I handed him the fee displayed on the meter.

"Thank you. I'm sorry for your loss, I wish you both well," the driver said.

"Thank you," I replied, picking up Ben's car seat. I took the house key from my shoulder bag, unlocked the door and placed the car seat on the floor in the hallway. Ben slept soundly on. After the taxi had driven off I went back out to close the gates. I felt safer with them locked. The burglary still left me feeling uneasy. Back inside I locked the front door. I carried Ben to the living room and placed him in the middle of the floor, unsure of what to do. Carrier bags full of baby clothes, a blanket, baby monitors, bottles, baby milk formula, nappies, wipes and soft toys still lay on the sofa where I'd left them after my earlier shopping trip. I'd tried to make sure I had all the essentials before going back to the hospital to collect Ben. I'd ordered a cot, bottle steriliser, Moses basket, play-mat and a baby mobile for next day delivery. I could never have carried it all.

He looked comfortable in his car seat, tiny face screwed up in sleep, but I really wanted to hold him. I unfastened his straps and picked him up. He squirmed, but once I'd sat back on the sofa he slept peacefully in my arms. I took out my phone (still turned off) from my shoulder bag and turned it on. I desperately needed to phone Dad but dreading what he'd say. I hoped he wouldn't shout or demand I take Ben back to the hospital or claim that he wasn't his son. I looked at Ben. He resembled Bobby as a newborn, but then all babies look the same. I'd had little reason to trust Kate, but had really believed her claim she was carrying Dad's child. I looked at Ben again, almost certain she'd told the truth. I called Dad, ignoring all the missed texts on my phone; they'd all be from Mum or Gary. After a couple of rings he picked up.

"Dad?" My chest felt tight. It hurt.

"Lorna. What's wrong?" He'd never consider I'd phone just for a chat.

"Dad, Kate's dead." My heart had frozen waiting for his reply.

"Kate ... Kate, with the gang ... last week?" His voice was controlled.

"Yes."

"My Kate?" That was unexpected.

"Yes, Dad."

"And ... the baby?" His voice was still controlled but I knew my Dad, even thousands of miles apart.

"I'm holding your son right now."

"You're holding him?"

"Yes. He was born last night. He's healthy."

"Are you at the hospital?"

"No, I'm at your house."

"Lorna ..."

"Please come home." I cut him short.

"Lorna, you're at my house with Kate's baby?"

Yes, with your son. Don't worry Dad, I've got everything I need. The hospital knows. I've got legal responsibility until you get home."

"Kate is really dead?"

"Yes. I saw her Dad. I'm so sorry."

"What happened?"

"I think you should come home."

"I need to know what happened to her."

"When you get home."

"Lorna. Tell me what happened." He was growing impatient.

"She wouldn't go to the hospital, worried they'd take the baby away. She phoned me last night and I took the train up to meet her. She was going to meet me at your house but the code was changed."

"I changed it last week after the burglary."

"I thought as much. I told her to go to the hospital but she wouldn't listen. She'd tried going through the woods, like she'd done a few weeks ago, to open the gate from the inside to let me in when I got here. She was in labour, the night was cold. She never made it through the woods." I took a deep breath. "She gave birth in the woods. I heard the baby crying. She was unconscious and bleeding heavily when I found her. She'd wrapped the baby in her coat. I took him and got out of the woods ... I couldn't carry Kate. I still had the key to your house so went inside to get help. I went with the baby to the hospital. A paramedic, police and fire crews searched the woods for Kate. They found her body ... there was nothing they could do." I heard him crying. He never cried. I hadn't thought I'd feel sorry for him but my heart burst with grief for him.

"It's my fault," he said.

"It's not." In as much as I could blame him it was the last thing he needed to hear.

"You know it is. I can't look after her son."

"Your son, Dad. Your son."

"I can't do it. I failed Bobby. You've told me what a terrible dad I am. That kid will be better off in care. I can't look after it."

"Dad! Get on a flight home and see your son. I promised Kate I'd look after him. She died because she didn't want to see her baby in care. I'm not going to let you give him away."

"I failed Kate."

"This is your chance to put that right. You're not going to fail her son." I'd never before felt fury like this. I looked down at Ben and knew I wouldn't let Dad give him away.

"Lorna, I can't be a single parent. I can't look after a baby on my own."

"I'll help you, Grandma and Grandad can help. You left Mum with Bobby when he was newborn. She coped, and so will you." He went silent.

"Dad, just come home and see your son."

"Okay. I'll book a flight home."

"Good, I'll see you soon."

"See you soon, Lorna."

I hung up. Ben had started crying.

"That was your dad on the phone. You'll meet him soon." He answered with more crying. "Yeah, I'd be crying too." I rummaged in the bag for bottles and baby formula then put him back in the car seat while I went into the kitchen to make his bottle. I felt calmer feeding him, the sound of him guzzling on the bottle quite soothing.

"When Dad sees you he'll love you. It just might take him a little time. I won't let him give you up." I talked while he was drinking. I'm glad I'd remembered to buy a bib; more milk went down his front.

I left him overnight in his car seat next to my bed. He looked adorable in a teddy bear night-suit and I'd wrapped him in a blanket. I'd sent Mum a text, nothing much, just that I was safe and would be home soon and explain everything. I ignored her calls. It would have been impossible to explain over the phone. I'd rather tell her in person. Dad had also sent me a text asking how I was, which I suppose was nice of him. I didn't sleep much, kept checking on Ben and worrying about Mum, also thinking about Kate. My burns stung but I felt a certain triumph at having escaped Declan's grasp. The woods and the fire wouldn't leave my mind despite being exhausted from two nights with little sleep. My mind was too traumatised to let me sleep. When I shut my eyes I'd feel the flames and think of Lynette's sister and nephew, the little boy called Ben. And when the fire wasn't burning the cold came back; the cold and the trees that had killed Kate. I preferred lying with eyes open, listening to Ben breathe, knowing that at that exact moment in time I was safe. He woke up several times and I fed him. One occasion I fell asleep feeding him but his scream soon woke me - the bottle had slipped from his mouth.

When Ben woke again sometime around six in the morning for a feed I decided to stay up. I curled up on the sofa and watched TV with him in my arms. I went for breakfast as the sun was starting to rise and watched the day start from behind the huge glass windows. I found myself staring at the distant woods. My mind wandered back there. Tears rolled down my cheeks. I wasn't crying over Kate. I'd barely known her, besides, she'd betrayed me just the week before. I was crying because I hadn't saved her. And I knew I was putting my Mum through hell. I didn't know if Dad would ever love Ben enough to keep him. And the five year old Ben at number 4 ...? I couldn't stop thinking about him. All was without a doubt my fault.

While getting dressed I heard a loud buzzing sound. I went downstairs to investigate and realised it was someone calling at the gates. I prayed it wasn't the midwife. Outside I saw a large truck and breathed a sigh of relief. The delivery man. He dropped off the boxes and parcels in the hallway, I signed a piece of paper and he went on his way. I closed the gates and the door before hunting through the baby stuff. I opened the play mat first and laid it out in the front room. It was bright and colourful with lots of differing textures. There was an arch that went over it with moving blocks, spinning mirrors and other colourful things that made a racket when hit or spun. Ben was far too young to play properly with it but it said *newborn* on the box so I laid him down on the mat. I hoped it would be a good sign for the midwife.

Next I set up the steriliser. I was running out of clean milk bottles. Ben cried the minute I left the room. After five minutes his screaming became too much so I went back to the living room and swivelled the play mat around to face the TV. I stayed with him for a couple of minutes. When I left he seemed happy, listening to some cookery programme. I tried setting up the Moses basket in the living room. The cradle was okay but the stand was flat packed. It took a lot longer to build than I'd thought it would. The midwife arrived soon after. I kicked all the packaging to one corner of the room before opening the gate. I hadn't had a chance to make the cot but I couldn't even lift the box. I'd leave that job for Dad.

The midwife was a lovely lady. She held Ben for a little while, asking questions about his feeding and sleeping. She was happy with the Moses basket and play-mat and stayed to watch me feed and change him. She asked quite a lot of questions about Dad. I said he was getting the plane home this evening, probably in the airport now, (a lie), but I didn't want her to have any doubts. She said she'd have to see my Dad, preferably within the week, but was otherwise happy. I felt so relieved when she'd left. I sent Dad a text to say the midwife had been and was happy. I hoped he'd be happy knowing his daughter was responsible enough to look after his son. I also asked him what time his flight home was.

A phone rang. For a second I thought it was mine, but mine was still in my hand. The sound was faint so I stood up to follow it. It was coming from Kate's bag, on the floor next to the sofa. I picked it up, found the phone - the caller was 'Jamie.' I answered.
"Kate?"
"Jamie." I replied, hoping he wouldn't realise.
"I'm in big shit Kate. You gotta help me." His voice was rough.
"Kate can't help you anymore."
"What! Who is this?" He demanded.
"Someone who knew Kate."
"Where's Kate?"
"She's dead."

"What're you on about?"

"Kate's dead."

"No she aint!"

"She died last night."

"You're lying to me. She's making you lie." His voice was aggressive.

"I'm not. I'll give you the address of the hospital; you can go and see her body." My tone was harsh but I'd disliked him instantly.

"She's making you fucking lie!" He shouted.

"She's dead."

"She just doesn't want to help me. The stupid bitch. I'll find out she's lying. She'll come back to me one day."

"Why would she go back to you?"

"She always does."

"Not this time."

"So, how come she was trying to help me? She ran away and left me for a year, but now she's trying to help me. She's only doing it to get back with me." I didn't know if this guy's ego was incredibly large or if Kate really was that stupid, but it didn't matter anymore.

"Kate died last night." I told him the name of the hospital and told him to phone them if he didn't believe me. "She can't help you." I hung up.

I switched her phone off and put it back in her bag. Dad could bin her few possessions if he wanted to but I wouldn't feel right doing it. I hoped Kate hadn't been considering going back to Jamie with her baby. And, as harsh as I'd sounded, if that had been her plan maybe her death had been for the best. The thought of Ben growing up with that Jamie, surrounded by drugs and those men who'd held a knife to my throat terrified me. She'd escaped for a reason, she couldn't have gone back there with a baby? However, the phone call had settled my mind slightly. From what Kate had said, Jamie was the last person she'd been with before Dad, and Jamie had said he hadn't seen her for a year. I was now almost certain Ben was my brother. I hoped Dad would think the same.

I boiled some pasta for some sort of meal, even though there was no sauce ... the cupboards were pretty much bare. Dad finally got back to me saying his flight had been cancelled due to bad weather, so he wouldn't be flying until tomorrow. I went online to check the weather in America, certain he was making up an excuse. I clicked on the weather app. A full moon sign appeared next to the temperature indicator. It took me a moment to realise what that actually meant and then I clicked, there was going to be a full moon that night! I double-checked online to make sure there was going to be a full moon. Every site I visited confirmed it. I couldn't wait a moment longer. I rushed to the living room.

"You've got to do your sister a big, big favour tonight, Ben." He slept on. "You're going to help me get rid of Declan, but we've got a long journey. So, please be good for me, then you'll get to meet your brother Bobby. He'll be very excited to meet you. Plus, you get to meet my Mum and Gary." (They would be anything but excited at seeing him.) I checked out train times, planned my route home, called for a taxi then packed a bag for Ben. I was soon on the train home.

The trip to the station had been uneventful, Ben asleep the whole time. Wrapped up in a blanket in his car seat he looked so peaceful and content. I wished I was asleep too, but I had much to do before my head could finally touch a pillow, like travel across half the country. I was shattered but didn't want to sleep in case I missed my stop. The sun set and the faint outline of the moon began to show ... definitely a full moon: I felt so relieved ... the gateway into the afterlife, and before it set would be destroying an evil soul that still roamed this Earth. Kate would already be there. Was she looking down at me ... at her son ... what did she think about me naming him? What did she think of what we were about to do?

Ben woke up on our second train. I'd prepared some milk for him before we'd left. It was cold, but that couldn't be helped. At first he spat it out, but after several attempts he finally drank. I was conscious of other passengers gawking. They'd think Ben was my baby, and I an irresponsible parent bringing a new-born baby on a late night train. It must have been an odd sight. I still hated them for staring though. The last ten minutes of the journey he cried and screamed - embarrassing. He needed changing but until we arrived at the station I could do nothing. I knew he'd woken people up ... tough. Fed and changed he fell asleep on the next train. I was nervous about going home and anxious about what Declan would try. But the train pulled into the last stop so soon. I'd hated how the journey had taken so long when I'd needed to get to Kate quickly, and tonight, when I'd have happily travelled to the edge of the universe, I was back home so soon. I picked up Ben, now snugly tucked up in his blanket and hooked the bag over my shoulder. The doors opened and I stepped out into the cold night. I wanted to get Ben indoors quickly. I walked away from the lit platform, down the dark back street towards the centre of town. I was shivering. Stars were out and the moon still shone, but the wind bit at my face. I tucked the blanket tighter around Ben.

I reached the high street in a couple of minutes. Shops were closed but the bars were open; the first few drunks of the night staggering about, shouting. Young adult groups wandering from bars to clubs, laughing and yelling. Not a place for a baby. A couple of police officers patrolled the street. Despite their presence I still felt vulnerable. I took the first turning down a side street to the taxi ranks. The place looked so different at night. My footsteps echoed, like in a ghost town. The noise of the high street fading fast. I was paranoid about being watched. I knew I was being stupid.

Ben's car seat weighed down in my arms, and although he was only tiny, by the time I'd found my way to the taxis via backstreets, my shoulder ached. I opened the door of the first one, my hands numb with cold. I wasn't wearing makeup and must have looked like a kid again. I gave the taxi driver my address and fastened Ben in. I went and sat in the back as well, behind the driver's seat.

"You're a bit young to be walking around town this time of night, aren't you?" He asked, accusingly.

"I've just come from the station."

"Been drinking with your mates I suppose. I doubt any of the bouncers would let you in, then again, I've seen kids younger than you coming out of them bars." I didn't bother telling him I was eighteen.

"I haven't been drinking, I've got a baby with me."

"Says it all."

"He's not mine!" I retorted, appalled. He scoffed at me. He didn't see the look I gave him. I counted to ten to calm myself down, no good getting angry or back-chatting, he'd only kick me out, then how would I get home then? We sat in silence for a couple of minutes until Ben woke up and started crying. I tried giving him some more milk but he didn't want it and there was nothing else I could do while in the car.

"Can't you shut the bloody thing up?"

"No, I forgot to ask the midwife where the off button is."

"Bloody immature kids, getting pregnant ... can't even look after themselves, never mind their sprogs."

"I've told you. He's not mine." Ben was screaming.

"Just drop me off here." I raised my voice. It was still a couple of streets to go but I didn't care. Getting out of the disgusting taxi and calming Ben was more urgent. My ears were ringing. I gave him the fare and, purely to be awkward, waited for the 10p change. I closed the door rather loudly and unfastened Ben from the other seat. The driver revved his engine loudly before driving off, making Ben howl even more. I dropped my bag to the ground and unfastened him from the car seat. He stopped crying the moment I picked him up. I put the bag in the car seat and carried both in the crook of my elbow. Ben, thankfully, lay still. I was terrified he'd start squirming, slip from his blanket and I'd drop him. I reached the end of my street. I couldn't yet see my house, but number 4 was visible ... a blacked out shell. Police tape lined its perimeter. I crossed the road. If Ben hadn't been in my arms I'd probably have ducked under and walked straight up to the house. I forced myself to look away and turned towards my own home. No lights in the windows, curtains closed. They'd be in there, Mum still awake trying to fool the world that everything was okay.

There was one more thing I had to do before going home. I looked skywards. Stars shone. The full moon, brighter than anything in the night, almost dousing the orange glow from the street lights. I'd come all the way back for this, but what exactly was I supposed to do? Conditions were perfect. Full moon, a new-born baby. I was near to where he'd died. But how to destroy him? How did it work? Would it just happen or did I have to say something? Would I know if it had happened? Would I feel it, would Ben feel anything? I had no idea. Feeling rebellious, I put down the car seat, ducked under the police tape and took a few steps towards the house. Going inside would be foolish, especially if carrying Ben. I edged around the side hurrying down the narrow path to the back garden. I had a sickening feeling the wall would collapse on top of us. I shouldn't be here, this was reckless. If anything happened? I could taste the smoke, air drying my throat. I shouldn't be here with any baby, never mind new-born. But Ben was able to stop it here, where it all began. I walked to the back door - still open - the white plastic now black with soot. I couldn't see inside, everything was black. Not much to see anyway.

Standing outside the house was dangerous. The police had taped it off as unsafe. Above all, it was a crime scene, and I was guilty enough without more evidence. If they found my footprints in the soot it would look more than suspicious. I'd been lucky so far. But what if I needed to go to the bottom of the stairs - the exact spot where he'd died? If I went inside I might increase the death count to four, and I couldn't risk Ben's life. Forensics had been inside since the fire, bodies had been removed and the house hadn't collapsed on *them*, but that didn't mean it was safe. Why had I named him Ben? To stop the guilt? I looked down at the tiny face on my shoulder. I couldn't believe I was about to risk his life. He hadn't moved or made a sound since I'd ducked under the tape but his eyes were wide open. Had he sensed something? I placed one foot on the kitchen floor.

"I wouldn't do that if I were you, Lorna."
I almost jumped out of my skin. I whipped my foot back onto solid ground, needing something to steady me. I'd almost dropped Ben.
"Now, step away from the house." His voice was calm and assertive. I didn't move.
"Don't be stupid, Lorna." My mind went blank, the shock had wiped away everything. He couldn't read me.
"How do I do it?" He knew what the question meant.
"You're not a murderer, Lorna."
"Yeah, I am. You turned me into one." I was speaking out loud. I needn't have, but felt more in control that way.
"And you're haunted by it. You're riddled with guilt, you don't need any more."

"How can I kill someone who's already dead?"

"Murder is a terrible thing Lorna. You've done some pretty bad things recently. You've changed so much. But to knowingly kill me is an entirely different matter."

"You're already dead!" That infuriated him. I felt his temper rising.

"So, leave me in peace."

"You had your chance at peace."

"You don't need revenge. You're different from me."

"Not anymore. And you caused that. You're to blame for your own fate. It's your fault you died. Your fault if I destroy you."

"You wouldn't."

"Why not? You can't threaten me anymore. Give me one reason why I shouldn't do it."

"You don't know how to." True. So true.

"I'll just have to try then." I looked up at the moon, then into Ben's blue eyes.

"Don't do it, Lorna." He rushed his words, distracting my attention. This was my one chance, this night only. It had to be done. No matter what he says to me, he won't stop until his wife's dead. No matter the cost.

"I'll go. Please, Lorna. I'll leave. I give you my word I'll leave you and never come back. Just don't do this. I was a human once. Imagine me how I was. You wouldn't kill a person. This is worse than murder. This will be it. The end. Full stop. Over. Gone. Please don't do this. I've done bad things, but Ben, my sister-in-law, they went on, *they're happy together. Just give me this one chance to go. I will leave you be. You can live a good life. You don't want this hanging over you the rest of your life, you've tarnished my memory enough. Don't ruin me."* I'd warned myself it would happen. He'd try and persuade me not to. I couldn't let that happen. I was stronger. He couldn't get away with what he'd done. He ranted on and on. My brain felt like it would implode. My thoughts mixed with his. I spoke out loud.

"He needs to die." I looked at the moon. "Remove Declan's spirit from this earth. I offer his life for Ben's. Get him out of my mind. Tear him apart. Make him hurt. Vengeance and justice for what he's done. Banish his evil from this world." I raised my voice with each word, to drown out his moans and cries. My knees buckled. I crashed to the ground, throwing myself backwards to protect Ben. Pain. Ben rolled from my shoulder onto the floor. He made no sound. My head was splitting, the noise horrendous, the pain excruciating. Declan railed inside my head, shrieking and screeching - deafening. I cupped my head in my hands. My forehead split open. Tears streamed down my face.

Chapter 11

Everything ceased instantly. The drawn out echo of his last scream. Then silence. The memory of the pain was all that remained. I lay on my back catching my breath. I hunched up and looked down at Ben. He stared up, lying motionless. The white glow of the moon reflected in his black pupils. For one terrible moment I thought he was dead. My hand reached out for his cheek. Then he looked at me intently, his body still rigid. Something had changed. He blinked and that look vanished, he was an innocent baby once more. I could hear him gurgle.

"It's over Ben. It's all over." I laughed, a grin spread from ear to ear. I'd destroyed Declan's soul. Never again would he haunt this Earth. He was dead ... well and truly.

I picked Ben up and got up onto my own two feet. Feeling elated I headed back around the side of the house, ducked back under the tape, picked up the car seat and crossed the road. I stood at the top of the drive, looking at my home. Ben squirmed so I shushed and rocked him. But I still couldn't find it within myself to take one more step. Less than five metres from home, yet as difficult as five thousand. I didn't know what to do. I found the front door key in my shoulder bag. I couldn't stay out here forever, and I couldn't go back. Ben shouldn't be in this cold anyhow. I'd have to face them sometime, now or later made no difference. What would I say? How would I explain Ben?

I took a deep breath and walked to the front door. Ever so slowly I placed the key into the lock and twisted it ... click. I turned it further, pulled it out and put it back in my bag. I don't know whether he could feel my tension or not, but Ben was still. I realised I'd been holding my breath. My palm closed around the door handle. I pushed it down, grimacing at the noise. I didn't want them to hear me, not yet. I opened it ever so carefully and stepped inside ... onto a lump on the floor. It squealed. I jumped and stumbled back out of the door, dropping the car seat. The contents of the bags spilled out all over the ground. Holding onto Ben for dear life I managed to stay upright.

"Lorna!" Bobby yelled.

"Shush Bobby. Quiet." Too late. I stepped back in the house, giving

Bobby a one-armed hug.

"I missed you so, so much," I told him.

"I missed you too." He tried snuggling up further but Ben was in the way.

"Careful Bobby, you'll hurt Ben." In the dim light I saw his confused face looking up at me. Then he looked down and saw Ben. He raised a small hand and touched Ben's cheek - all he could see in the bundle of blankets. I knelt down level with Bobby, looking at the baby in my arms, his expression gentle.

"A baby." Bobby whispered in awe.

"Your brother."

Footsteps sounded. Mum and Gary hurrying down the stairs. My heart skipped a beat as I saw the two figures approaching me.

"Bobby, what on earth are you doing down here?" Mum asked sternly. She switched on the light. She wore her white dressing gown with red love hearts and fluffy slippers. Gary stood just behind her in jogging bottoms and a green T-shirt. I watched the colour vanish from their faces as they looked at me, expressions moving between anger, shock and disbelief. No one spoke. Bobby looked from me to Mum and back to me, his little face radiating fear. Ben gave a little cough and Bobby shuffled away from me, edging closer to the wall. I looked down at Ben (he'd coughed a second time) and caught Mum and Gary's eyes riveted to the baby in my arms. I stood up cautiously, cradling Ben, feeling self-conscious and stupid. I stepped back towards the door, Mum and Gary just stared, still saying nothing.

"I'm so sorry." I whispered, my voice shaky. I waited a moment or two for a reply (which didn't come) then spoke again. "I had to go. It was an emergency. I had no choice." Still silence. "I'll explain everything."

"I know you will. And fast." Mum glared. Gary said nothing. I'd hoped to find some friendliness in his eyes, but none.

"That … thing … it's not yours, is it?" It was so ridiculous and impossible I laughed. I stared at them in total bewilderment.

"Answer your mother, Lorna." Gary instructed. I looked at him.

"You don't actually think … you cannot believe …?" I was speechless.

"Answer your mother! Is that child yours?"

"No! Of course not!" I glared at them, shaking with fury. "How can you

127

think that? It would have been a bit more obvious wouldn't it?" I raged at them. I was suddenly so angry.

"So, who's is it then?" *It. It.* I wanted to scream until they began listening to their words.

"He's not an *it!* He's my brother!" I shouted so loud, all my emotions of the past flooded out. Bobby cowered back. I whipped around and stepped back outside, slamming the door behind me. Ben cried. I held him close. I shouldn't have done that with him in my arms. I was about halfway down the drive when I heard the door open again. It was Gary.

"Lorna," he called. "Calm down. Come back inside. You need to explain to us what on earth is going on." I let him lead me inside, into the front room. I ruffled Bobby's hair as I passed him then sat down without looking at Mum, seated beside Gary on the other sofa. Bobby shuffled in beside Mum. The last thing I'd wanted was to scare him and I felt terrible. I shushed Ben, still crying though not as much.

"His name's Ben," I said, "He's Dad's son."

"Your dad's in ..."

"America. I know. He's catching a flight home tomorrow."

"I didn't know he had a girlfriend?" Mum said.

"He doesn't but he got a girl pregnant."

"*Girl?*"

"She was about twenty."

"*Twenty!*" Mum exclaimed, disgusted.

"Where is she?" Gary asked.

"Dead." I let that sink in before continuing. "I tried to help her. When Dad found out she was pregnant he dumped her. She had no family, no friends. I had to help. She phoned me the other night to say she was in labour. She wouldn't go to the hospital without me so I had to go to Dad's. There was no time to explain." I went on to tell them everything. They listened, horrified but attentive. I was glad they didn't interrupt. I explained how I'd first seen Kate, about Dad's house with the gates and the woods. I told them what I knew about Kate, the woods and fetching Ben from the hospital.

"I lied to you last week." I admitted. "I wasn't going to Dad's to get my history coursework. I went to see Kate. Something happened that day which made Dad change the code on the locks. There is something else I should have told you about." I had purposely edited this from my story but I thought they'd need to know.

"Kate's ex was in trouble with this gang. He'd lost them a lot of money. She'd said she'd help him ... gave the gang the address to Dad's. She knew he was away in America and led them to the house: but I'd kept the gates open to let *her* in. There were three men on motorbikes; they burgled the house."

"When you were in the house?"

"Yes."

"And Kate knew you were there?"

"Yes."

"Did they hurt you?"

"Not really."

"Lorna. Did they hurt you?" Mum's tone was deadly serious.

"They had knives. One of them grabbed me, another threatened me with the knife. But the alarms went off when they tried to break into Dad's study so they ran."

"Oh my God."

"I phoned the police, had Kate arrested. That's why she wouldn't go to the hospital without me. She was linked to this gang and had no permanent address. She thought social services would take the baby away from her."

"You should have told us." Gary said.

"You were going through enough. Mum had lost the baby."

"You're my daughter. You tell me. Anything could have happened to you." Mum was crying. "No matter what's going on you always come and talk to me. You're more important than anything else."

"We could have helped." Gary said.

"You couldn't have. I was fine."

"You've been through so much on your own. You didn't tell us about Declan. You shouldn't have kept us in the dark."

"It's over now. There's nothing you could have done." It was such a relief hearing that it really was all over.

"You said the baby is called Ben?" Gary asked, a detail that had slipped my mind while telling them the story. "It wasn't your fault. There was nothing you could have done." He was of course referring to the older Ben, the child who'd died in the fire.

"I know. I said Ben to the midwife, I don't know why. Dad will probably change his name anyway." I had loads more questions to answer before they let me go off to bed. They wanted to know every detail. I understood why. Bobby stayed mostly silent, not really understanding, and Ben had fallen asleep in my arms.

"When is your dad coming home?" Mum asked.

"Tomorrow. I think. He was meant to be coming home today but apparently his flight was cancelled." Mum gave me '*the look*'. She knew as well as I it was probably one of Dad's lies.

"We're going to have to take Ben back to your Dad."

"I know. I shouldn't have brought him here. I didn't know what else to do." I'd only brought him here for the full moon - quite selfish.

"It's okay, we wanted you back home. I'll drive you both up tomorrow, in time for him coming home."

"Thanks."

As Mum was shooing Bobby back to bed he said to me, "I crept downstairs when Mum and Gary had gone to bed. I sat waiting for you but I fell asleep. I wanted to see you when you came home. I knew you would come home." I felt my eyes fill with tears and my heart swelled with love for my innocent, cheeky brother. Gary ruffled his hair and Mum gave him a hug.

"Thank you Bobby. You didn't have to do that."

Taking Gary to Dad's the next day felt quite bizarre, as though my two differing worlds had combined yet didn't quite fit together.

"It's left here." We were on the country road close to the lane.

"You sure?" He looked suspiciously at the narrow track in between the trees.

"Positive. Left here. There'll be some gates on the left somewhere down here." He drove down the lane carefully until we reached the gates. I read out the new code that Dad had sent me earlier that day. The gates opened and Gary drove through them up to this grand house in his rusty, red, ten year old car.

"Wow." I think he felt slightly intimidated by its size. I'd purposely '*forgotten*' detailing to them about Dad's house.

"When you said about the gates and the grounds with woods I guessed your Dad lived in a posh place, but nothing like this." I didn't know what to say, so I got out of the car and unfastened Ben. I felt uncomfortable walking into the house with Gary next to me, carrying my bags. He didn't belong here. At home I managed to forget about this house. It was just a big house, not a home. I didn't want to always be comparing what we had to what Dad had. I liked our three-bed semi and didn't want them feeling that he was better than them in any way.

"Your mum has asked me to stay with you until your Dad arrives." Gary said from the doorway, where he'd dropped my bags.

"Okay. Come in and sit down."

"I don't want to intrude." Gary had never met Dad but had heard enough about him to dislike him. I knew he felt awkward.

"I'm sure he'll understand. Ben stayed the night at our's and kept everyone awake through most of it." I made us a black coffee. There was no milk. Gary went for a walk around the grounds, purely to get out of the house I think. I sorted out some bottles for Ben and put away the new clothes I'd bought him. A text from Dad said he'd be home by eight that evening. We sat on the stools at the kitchen bar waiting. I don't think Gary wanted to sit in the front room looking as though he'd made himself at home. He'd offered to sit in the car. I wouldn't have it. He was the one who'd brought Dad's son home. We sat in silence. I was beginning to feel nauseous. I'd be in so much trouble.

I was playing with Ben on my knee when the front door opened. He'd been awake for the past twenty minutes. I'd sort of hoped he'd still be asleep. Surely Dad wouldn't shout with a sleeping baby in the house.

"Lorna."

I stood up and pushed my chair in. Gary did the same. I went to greet him in the hallway. Gary stayed put. Black stubble covered Dad's jaw and he had dark circles under his eyes. Although still smartly dressed it diminished his professional and domineering exterior.

"Hi Dad." His eyes fixed on Gary.

"You must be Liz's partner, Gary isn't it?" The atmosphere thickened.

"Yes. She asked me to stay with Lorna until you were home. I'll leave now." He took a step forward.

"No, no ... I'd like you to stay." They were being strictly formal, trying to figure each other out. Ben and I seemed invisible, not that I minded. Gary nodded.

"Lorna has spoken of you. She said you're good to Bobby."

"I try to be."

"I'm sorry to have troubled you with the baby and you having to travel up here."

"It's been no trouble." Gary had said to me earlier that, living with two of Dad's kids, having another stay for one night was no problem.

"I do apologize." This was not how Dad usually spoke. An awkward silence while they stood looking at each other, then Ben sneezed. Both men looked at Ben. Dad didn't move, glued to the spot, as though scared of the baby. I walked over to him.

"This is Ben." I held Ben forward, offering him for Dad to take but he froze, standing motionless, looking at his son. Nothing changed his expression, blank. And then something happened I'd never thought possible - a tear rolled from his left eye. A tear from his right followed. He was crying! If Gary had felt embarrassed earlier it was nothing compared to now. He was looking down at something highly interesting on the spotless floor.

"Kate's eyes." Dad whispered, his voice thick.

"Kate's eyes." I repeated.

"I killed her, didn't I?"

"It wasn't your fault. You were in America."

"I let her down."

"You can change that." I passed Ben into his arms. He looked terrified but soon smiled as he watched Ben staring up at him with bright eyes. "Hello little one." Ben's eyes screwed up and he began to cry. Dad looked shocked and handed him straight back to me.

"I'll get him a bottle."

"If you'll excuse me for a minute." Dad went upstairs. After a few minutes he came back, his hair slightly wet. I figured he'd splashed water over his face. He went over to the fridge, took out two cans and passed one to Gary.

"Thanks."

"No problem." Dad said, perched on a bar stool near Gary. I sat on one between them.

"What's that on your hand?" Dad asked. I looked at the hand holding the baby bottle, the dressing still on. In the kitchen light it was clearly visible.

"It's nothing," I said defensively, glaring at Gary.

"What did you do?" Dad asked, suspiciously.

"There was a fire at the neighbour's house." I said, looking at Ben. "Gary will explain, I'm going to put Ben down." Gary nodded. I walked into the living room and laid Ben in his Moses basket. I sat for a while watching him sleep. I didn't want to go straight back into the kitchen. Eventually I figured I couldn't hide much longer and went back.

"I have a hero for a daughter," Dad repeated, smiling.

"No you don't," I retorted, rather too fiercely.

"You ran into a burning building and saved someone's life."

"I don't want to talk about it." I felt a bit like a stroppy teenager but I wanted to forget about the fire, about the people I killed.

"You could have told me."

"I didn't want to talk about it. It's over now."

"You should have told me about Declan. He assaulted you, threatened you. I want to know these things. " He'd probably have been the last person I'd have told.

"You told him about Declan?" I asked Gary.

"That man is lucky he's dead," said Dad.

"Your Mum insisted. She said I had to make sure you hid nothing."

"I wasn't going to."

"Like you didn't hide from us that those men held a knife to your throat?"

"The police gave me a full account of the burglary last week. They said exactly what you told them," Dad told me. They'd really discussed a lot while I'd been out of the room.

"I told you and Mum they'd threatened me with knives," I said to Gary.

"You didn't tell us they'd held a knife to your throat."

"Mum was already upset, she didn't need the details."

"I can't believe Kate brought those men here. You were in the house."

"Dad, there's something else. When I first came to the house and saw Kate I sneaked back out to talk to her." I told him about taking Kate inside for the night, about how I'd kept in contact with her.

"I didn't come back here for my history coursework. I came to see Kate. The gates were open because I was waiting for Kate to get here."

"I can't believe she deceived you like that."

"Nor I. But she's dead now. We need to move on."

"I want to know what happened the night she died." I explained everything, from the phone call to her death. It was hard telling it again. "I couldn't leave her in the woods. I needed to get help but couldn't have gone back into the woods. I think she'd have wanted me to have stayed with Ben."

"I think so too. It was lucky for Ben you were there. And I think he might need you for a few more days. Will you teach me how to look after him ... stay for a little while?" He asked me, but looked at Gary for permission.

"I've got college."

"A few days won't matter, surely?"

"I doubt it." I looked at Gary.

"Yeah, it's up to you."

"I'll phone Mum and let her know."

"Okay, I better be off home now," Gary announced.

"It was good meeting you," said Dad, and held his hand out. Gary shook it.

"And you."

"Thank you, again, for all you've done. Lorna has told me how Bobby loves you. I hope you and Liz will give me another chance with him ... if Bobby agrees to see me."

"I'm sure something can be arranged soon."

"Thank you." I walked Gary back to the car.

"Thanks for bringing us back here."

"No problem."

"Tell Mum not to worry."

"I think that'll be impossible now." He laughed.

"I didn't want to cause any trouble."

"I know, and what's happened is not your fault."

"Thank you for telling Dad about Declan. I know he needed to know, but I don't think I could have told him myself."

"You've been through a lot. I know you don't like talking about things and I didn't want you to have to re-live it in your head all over again."

"I know, thanks for talking to Dad. It couldn't have been easy for you."

"Everyone deserves a second chance."

"I think he knows he needs to step up this time."

"Hopefully. See you in a few days."

"Say hi to Bobby from me." I gave him a hug.

"He was very worried about you. He knew something was wrong."

"Bless him."

"I'll be off now. But if there's ever something you don't think you can talk to your Mum and Dad about, talk to me."

"Thanks. I will. Mum and Bobby ... and me, are lucky to have you." Hugs again.

"Bye." I waved. Dad had taken the box with the cot to Ben's bedroom upstairs. We sat trying to build the flat-pack cot. It took ages. Neither of us knew what to do but had a laugh and a good chat. I could feel myself starting to forgive, feeling comfortable talking to him.

"Lorna, I'm going to take a paternity test," he announced while screwing one of the last wooden beams into place.

"I understand."

"In my heart I know he's my son. But I can't live with doubt."

"That's okay."

A few weeks later I was playing with Bobby and his new toys round Dad's house when the postman rang the doorbell. Dad came back inside holding a letter in a vice-like grip, apprehension etched on his face, in his eyes. He opened the envelope slowly and deliberately. Gradually the look of concentration eased into happiness as he read.

"He's my son!" He beamed.

"I never doubted it."

Lauriane Povey is 21 years old and studies International Relations at Durham University. She is also a councillor within Stockton Borough Council, one of the youngest in the country when elected in 2015. Around her studies and work, Lauriane tries to find time to write and plan the many books she hopes to write. To find out more about Lauriane please visit her website at www.laurianepovey.co.uk

www.ingramcontent.com/pod-product-compliance
Lightning Source LLC
Chambersburg PA
CBHW060620130626
46555CB00002B/589